For His Name's Sake

Other Books by Debbie Viguié

The Psalm 23 Mysteries

The Lord is My Shepherd
I Shall Not Want
Lie Down in Green Pastures
Beside Still Waters
Restoreth My Soul
In the Paths of Righteousness

The Kiss Trilogy

Kiss of Night
Kiss of Death
Kiss of Revenge

Sweet Seasons

The Summer of Cotton Candy
The Fall of Candy Corn
The Winter of Candy Canes
The Spring of Candy Apples

Witch Hunt

The Thirteenth Sacrifice
The Last Grave
Circle of Blood

For His Name's Sake

Psalm 23 Mysteries

#7

By Debbie Viguié

Published by Big Pink Bow

For His Name's Sake

Copyright © 2013 by Debbie Viguié

ISBN-13: 978-0615895529

Published by Big Pink Bow

www.bigpinkbow.com

This is a work of fiction. Names, characters, places, and incidents either are the product of the author's imagination or are used fictitiously. Any resemblance to actual persons, living or dead, is purely coincidental.

Dedicated to the fans who have loved and supported this series. Thank you all.

Thank you to everyone who helped make this book a reality, particularly Barbara Reynolds, Rick Reynolds and Calliope Collacott.

1

Cindy Preston was always slightly suspicious of Wednesdays. Wednesdays, the middle of the week when you could start celebrating a work week half-finished or nearly, were often the days when life threw you a curve ball and turned your perfectly ordinary week upside down and into something completely...different.

"Weird Wednesdays" was what her roommate and coworker Geanie often called them and Cindy had grown to agree with her. Just to make it that much more unpredictable, only some Wednesdays shook things up. Others were perfectly calm and quiet. Working as a church secretary could be stressful and unpredictable at times. Wednesdays were usually one of the days that the least number of people came into the office. Mondays and Tuesdays they were still dealing with issues from the weekend and Thursdays and Fridays ministry leaders were preparing for the new weekend. Wednesdays were usually quiet.

Except for when they weren't.

Like now.

"Weird Wednesday," she said out loud as she stared at herself in the full-length mirror. The image that stared back at her looked flushed, agitated. Why shouldn't she be all those things? After all, she was standing in the middle of a bridal shop wearing a wedding dress.

When she had woken up that morning nothing in the world could have prepared her for this.

"You look stunning," the owner of the store gushed.

"Thank you," Cindy mumbled, watching in the mirrors as her blush deepened.

"That dress fits you so perfectly," Geanie said. "And it looks like something right out of a fairy tale."

Cindy couldn't argue with that. The dress had a sweetheart neckline and a tightly fitted bodice. Short sleeves fluttered against her upper arms. Cascades of ruffles made their way down the dress and thousands of sequins and small crystals sparkled every time she moved. The train of the dress was nearly six feet long. It was a dress fit for a princess and wearing it she felt like one.

"So, will you be taking this one?" the owner asked.

Cindy couldn't even bring herself to look at the price tag on the dress, guessing that it was astronomically expensive. She glanced at Geanie who nodded enthusiastically. "Definitely. How long will it take to do any alterations? The wedding is in-"

"A week and a half, I remember. It's unusual to have such a rush job."

"Well, it was an emergency, it couldn't be helped," Cindy said, clearing her throat slightly.

"We can have the seamstress take measurements this evening and she should have everything done in a week, but it will cost more," the woman said.

"That's fine. This wedding has been a long time coming and everything has to be perfect," Geanie said brightly. "After all, a girl only marries her true love once."

Geanie glanced at her phone and winced. "Our lunch break is nearly over. We need to get back to work."

Cindy turned for one last wistful glance in the mirror. As she moved she could see the whole shop from the three angled mirrors in front of her, including the front windows. Outside she saw someone looking in, a man with his hand up to his eyes.

Cindy turned to look but he was gone.

"Joseph is a very lucky man," the owner of the shop said as she picked up the train so Cindy wouldn't get tangled in it as she stepped down off the dais she had been on.

"He doesn't know how lucky," Cindy said, flashing Geanie a quick grin.

Now it was Geanie's turn to blush. At least one of them was going to be a blushing bride.

"Are you sure you don't want to try the dress on before you buy it?" Cindy asked.

Geanie shook her head. "It's perfect, exactly what I wanted. Thank you for trying it on for me so I could get a good look at the whole thing. Besides, I'll be wearing it tonight while the seamstress pins everything."

Geanie's scramble to get a replacement wedding dress had all been brought about by the wedding planner accidentally having the last dress sent to Joseph's house that morning. Joseph had opened the box, realized what he was looking at and slammed it shut again before calling Geanie at work to tell her what had happened. The damage had been done, though. There was no way Geanie was walking down the aisle in a dress that Joseph had already had a glimpse of.

She had enlisted Cindy's help in emergency shopping and Cindy was just grateful she'd only had to try on three dresses instead of dozens. All the craziness with the wedding planning had had Geanie running so much that she'd dropped a couple of dress sizes and anything she tried on just hung on her so that she couldn't get a good idea of how it would look when it was actually fitted to her.

And just like that Cindy had gone from being the moral support to being the wedding dress model and she had to admit the whole experience had shaken her more than a little.

With Geanie's help she managed to get back out of the dress and she put her own clothes back on while Geanie paid for the gown. For just a moment she had stared at herself in that dress and wondered what it would be like to be the one getting married.

When she was a little girl she had spent hours thinking and talking about her future wedding with her sister Lisa. Since Lisa's death she hadn't given the whole topic much thought.

But now that she was thinking about it, she was finding it difficult to stop, especially when her thoughts drifted to a certain dark-haired rabbi.

"What is wrong with you?" she demanded of herself as she slipped on her shoes and prepared to join Geanie again. She was being ridiculous. There was nothing between her and Jeremiah, plain and simple. How could there be?

Yet every time she thought of him lately she felt a catch in her throat and she could swear her pulse would start to skitter out of control. She was being ridiculous.

"It's just Geanie and Joseph and all their wedding craziness, that's all," she whispered.

She took a deep breath and stepped out of the dressing room.

"All set," Geanie called and together they headed toward the door and Geanie's car waiting outside. Geanie was carrying a garment bag.

"You're not just leaving the dress here until tonight?"

"And risk something happening to this one? No. I'm going to have a hard enough time letting the seamstress take it at this point. Besides, I want to check it against my shoes and jewelry at home and make sure I still like how they'll work. I'd rather know now and not a week from now if I have to switch anything else around."

"It's a great dress," Cindy said as she got into the passenger seat.

"Thanks. You know, I think I'm going to like it better than the original one I picked out. How weird is that? It took me three months to find that first one."

"Maybe it was fate that Joseph saw the last one," Cindy teased.

"Don't joke, you know I believe in that kind of thing."

"I know."

"Now we have to go back to work. Weird Wednesday," Geanie said with a sigh.

Cindy thought of herself again in the dress. "Yes, yes it is," she agreed.

"I hope nothing else goes crazy this week now with the wedding."

Cindy remained quiet. In her experience when Weird Wednesdays hit, they were game changers which caused the rest of the week to be different, usually crazy.

"I'm glad your dress is already taken care of."

"Me, too." Cindy was going to be the maid of honor and her fuchsia satin gown had been safely tucked away in her closet for almost two months now.

"Joseph and the guys are getting their tux fittings tonight."

Which meant Jeremiah would be getting his tux. Cindy's breath caught in her throat at the thought. Any man looked good in a tuxedo but she just knew that Jeremiah was going to look amazing. He was going to be serving as Joseph's best man. It was something that he still seemed slightly surprised about.

It didn't surprise her at all. Joseph didn't have many close friends and she and Jeremiah had both saved him and his beloved award-winning dogs from murderous thieves. It made the four of them close even if Jeremiah didn't see it.

"You know if we're fast we can grab some to go sandwiches from the minimart down the street from the church," Geanie said.

Cindy's stomach rumbled at the thought. "Sounds good. I'd like to eat something before dinner." Minimart sandwiches were not high on her list of preferred foods but at least it was better than trying to work on an empty stomach.

Two minutes later Geanie pulled into the minimart. They hopped out of the car, ran inside, and quickly emerged with their sandwiches.

"Do you think Joseph will love the dress?"

"Are you kidding? You could wear a burlap sack and he'd love it," Cindy said.

She heard tires spinning on gravel and she turned to see a black sedan bearing directly down on them.

With a shout Cindy grabbed Geanie's arm and jumped back. The car swerved closer and she threw herself backward, landing with Geanie half in the doorway of the store. The sedan roared by, barely missing their feet.

She heard a shout from inside the store and a moment later the clerk was vaulting over them into the parking lot, his fist raised at the retreating car. He turned to them, his face ashen, and bent down.

"Are you ladies okay?"

Cindy nodded slowly as she sat up. "I'm okay, I think. Geanie, anything broken?"

"I'll let you know in a minute."

Geanie spoke so softly that alarm bells went off in Cindy's mind. Her roommate was typically anything but quiet. She turned and took a good look at her. Geanie's face was scrunched up in pain and she was holding her left elbow.

"I'm going to call the police," the clerk said.

"Did you get the license plate number?" Cindy asked.

"I sure did."

"Maybe you should call an ambulance, too."

"No, it's okay, I think I'm just bruised," Geanie protested.

"It wouldn't hurt to go to the hospital and have them check you out," Cindy said.

"No, no hospital. I'm fine and I don't have time to waste waiting for them to give me a bandage."

Geanie struggled to sit up and then flexed her left arm. "See, nothing broken, but I bet I'm going to have a heck of a bruise. My arm hit the ground first."

"Sorry," Cindy said.

"For what? Saving my life? Please, if it hadn't been for you that maniac would have run me down."

The clerk headed inside and Cindy could hear him talking as he called the police. She was grateful and more than a little surprised that he had managed to get the license plate number. Hopefully the police caught the maniac. The driver must have been drunk or something to drive so recklessly.

Unless they were trying to hit Geanie, the thought flashed through her mind. She dismissed it a minute later as ridiculous. No one on earth would want to harm Geanie, and besides, it wasn't like the minimart was a favorite hangout or anything. No, this had just been a case of wrong place wrong time. Fortunately neither of them had been really hurt.

Cindy pulled out her phone and put in a call to Sylvia, the business manager at the church, and let her know what had happened. She told Cindy that she would just put a closed sign on the office door and that in light of the circumstances she and Geanie should take the rest of the day off.

"What did she say?" Geanie asked when Cindy got off the phone.

"She said she's going to hang a sign on the office door that says 'Closed for Wedding Business'."

"Oh great," Geanie said, rolling her eyes.

"I'm pretty sure she was joking," Cindy said. With Sylvia it was sometimes hard to tell, but at least Cindy thought she was joking. The truth was that wedding fever had been starting to grip the whole church the last few days. It wasn't every day that a staff member married the church's wealthiest, most eligible bachelor. Gus, the music director at the church, had even taken to referring to it as the Royal Wedding. With the entire congregation invited it was going to be epically huge.

Two uniformed officers finally arrived and with a bit of disappointment Cindy realized she didn't know either of them. Thanks to all of the investigations she'd been involved in the past couple of years she'd met a lot of the local officers.

They took statements from her, Geanie, and the clerk. It was nearly an hour before they were finally able to leave.

Geanie drove them slowly home, still obviously sore. Fortunately they had driven in to work together so there was no need to stop at the church for Cindy's car. When they made it home and walked inside Cindy couldn't help but notice that the other woman was walking very stiffly.

"Maybe you should take a bath, it might help," Cindy suggested.

"That and a handful of aspirin," Geanie said with a strained smile.

"Are you sure you don't want me to take you to the doctor or the hospital, just to get checked out?"

"I'm sure, but thanks."

Geanie headed off to her room and Cindy glanced at the clock. It was half past two and she debated what to do with the rest of her afternoon. After a moment's hesitation she called Jeremiah's cell. She was about to ask if he wanted to have an early dinner. It went straight to voicemail, though, and she hung up without leaving a message.

She finally opted for doing laundry and watching a movie. It was boring, but the laundry needed to get done, and these might be the last few sane hours she had before the wedding consumed every waking moment.

A couple of hours later Geanie came into the family room looking immensely better than she had earlier. She was carrying the bag with her new dress in it and she was smiling again.

"Off to get it fitted?" Cindy asked.

"That's the plan. I'd ask if you wanted to come with, but it's going to be crazy boring."

"Yeah, I remember your last fitting," Cindy said with a smirk. "Hopefully this time you won't get jabbed with pins."

"In the ankle! What was with that?" Geanie demanded, clearly reliving her earlier injury.

"Have fun with that."

"I'll have fun later tonight."

"Doing something with Joseph?"

"No, he and the guys are doing the tux thing and you and I are going to be working on the wedding favors, remember?"

Cindy winced, having forgotten about that. It was a good thing she had done her laundry already. "Want me to see if I can get the other bridesmaids to come over tonight to help out?"

Geanie sighed. "My cousin doesn't get here until this weekend and Melissa and Veronica both said they're busy tonight."

I'll bet, Cindy thought privately. She plastered on a fake smile and out loud said, "Don't worry, we'll get them all done. They don't know what fun they're missing out on."

"I know, right? Besides, this is our one chance to get these done before everything gets really crazy."

Cindy wasn't sure she wanted to see what Geanie's idea of "really crazy" was. Still, she had agreed to be the maid of honor and this was all part of the package.

"Good luck, don't get stuck."

"I won't."

Cindy got up the moment the door closed. She had a couple more things she needed to straighten up around the house before the Royal Wedding took over completely.

She'd been cleaning the kitchen for about twenty minutes when her phone rang. Cindy snatched it up, hoping it was Jeremiah. She was disappointed when she saw that it was Geanie calling.

"Hey, everything okay?"

"In all the craziness, I forgot to bring my slip with me that I'm going to be wearing," Geanie said, sounding miserable.

"I can bring it to you."

"Thank you, I really appreciate it."

"That's what a maid of honor is for," Cindy said, forcing herself to sound cheerful to counter Geanie's gloominess.

"It's hanging in a garment bag to the left of my closet. It's that big, monstrous slip with all the layers."

"How can I forget? That thing is bigger than both of us combined. I'll grab it and be there in fifteen, maybe less."

"You're a life saver, thank you."

Cindy hung up, grabbed the slip and a minute later was in the car headed downtown. It was busy and she circled for five minutes looking for a parking place before she finally called Geanie.

"I'm here, I just can't park."

"That's okay, I'll run out and grab it from you and then you can just keep driving back home," Geanie said.

"Thanks, I haven't seen one car leave yet and I'm not the only one circling."

Cindy turned the corner and drove down the street where the entrance to the bridal shop was, still scanning for a parking spot. There were none, but up ahead she saw Geanie exit the store wearing the dress.

Cindy pulled as far to the side as she could so other cars could get around her and put on her hazard lights just for good measure. She unlocked the doors just as Geanie reached her.

Geanie opened the back door and reached for the bag with the slip with one hand while struggling to hold the gown up off the ground with the other.

"I'm surprised you're daring to wear that dress where prying eyes might see," Cindy teased.

"I didn't want to take it off just to put it back on again," Geanie said. "Thanks for this."

"Not a prob-"

A thunderous explosion ripped through the air and Cindy stared in horror as a fireball shot out of the front window of the bridal shop.

2

The shockwave threw Geanie against the car and a moment later debris was raining down all around them. Geanie disappeared from sight and Cindy threw open her car door and ran around to the other side, hands over her head to keep from getting hit by anything.

Geanie was slumped on the ground, face slack. Cindy couldn't tell what had knocked her unconscious but she knew she couldn't leave her there with bits of wood still falling. She could feel heat from the fire that was just steps away and seemed to be building in intensity. She braced herself for another explosion even as she reached down and grabbed hold of Geanie.

Through brute strength she got her off the ground and onto the backseat of the car before slamming the door shut and running back around and climbing in the driver's seat. Every instinct in her told her to drive, to get away before something else exploded.

The car was hemmed in, though. Other drivers had stopped all over the street, effectively blocking everyone as they gawked at the carnage. Black smoke was now pouring out of the building and engulfing parts of the street.

She felt a stinging on her back and reached up to feel a welt on her shoulder blade where something must have hit her while she was trying to move Geanie. She pounded the steering wheel in frustration. There was nowhere to go, nowhere to run. All she could do was pray that there wasn't another explosion.

She turned and looked in the back seat. Geanie was still out cold. With a start Cindy realized that part of the wedding dress was actually smoldering. She slapped at it with her hands, until it went out. She checked as best she could to see if there were any other embers burning their way through the dress but she couldn't see any.

A bruise was already forming on Geanie's cheekbone and Cindy wondered if something had hit her there or if it had been impact with the car that caused it. People began running everywhere. Patrons of the other businesses were flowing out into the streets. A couple of people were hauling buckets of water that would never even make a dent in the blaze that was going on.

Cindy forced herself to take several deep breaths. Now was not the time to go into shock. She studied the street again, trying to see if there was any way she could get them out of there. At last she realized that they weren't going anywhere without help.

~

Detective Mark Walters was sitting at his desk finishing up a report when his partner, Liam, stopped at his desk with an envelope in hand.

"What's up?" Mark asked.

Liam handed him the envelope. "This came for you. An officer found it just outside the building, laying on the ground. Someone must have dropped it."

Mark frowned as he took the envelope. That seemed odd to him. His name was on the front, but no address or any other markings. It definitely raised red flags for him. Then again, a lot of the digging he'd been doing lately could have led someone to want to communicate with him anonymously.

He grabbed a letter opener and sliced open the envelope. Inside was an index card with unfamiliar handwriting scrawled across it.

Ask him what his name is.

Mark stared at the note, struggling to comprehend its meaning. For the past ten months he'd been trying to discover the real identity of his former partner, Paul, who had been killed. In November he'd thought he'd discovered a clue while visiting a small town called Righteousness, something that would link Paul to a cult leader who had disappeared years before. The trail had been difficult to follow, though, and he'd grown desperate, casting his net far and wide to try and get any kind of information.

He reread the note. How could he possibly ask Paul his name? The man was dead and he hadn't been very forthcoming even when he was alive. He'd grown so frustrated in his search for the truth that he'd even enlisted the help of the church secretary and the rabbi since they seemed to be so good at solving impossible crimes. Even they hadn't been much help, though.

"Everything okay?" Liam asked.

Mark struggled with how to answer that. Liam knew a little bit about his investigation into Paul but he was

15

hesitant to bring his new partner completely on the inside for his own safety. Mark had been told months ago that the investigation was closed and he didn't want to involve Liam in matters that were strictly off the books and on their own time.

As it turned out he didn't have to answer at all.

"There's been a massive explosion downtown!" someone shouted.

Everywhere officers began to move. An explosion was trouble and downtown meant there were going to be a lot of people to question, a lot of ground to cover, especially if it turned out not to be an accident. Liam was already headed to the door when Mark jumped up to join him. They had just reached the car when Mark's phone rang.

A sudden sense of dread filled him as he pulled out the phone. "Hello?" he asked, answering it.

"Mark! It's Cindy, there's been an explosion!"

He closed his eyes. "Please tell me you're okay."

"I am, but Geanie's unconscious and I'm pretty sure the people inside the bridal shop are dead."

"Ambulances should be on their way."

"Mark, listen to me. I think someone's trying to kill Geanie."

Of course they were, because that was the world they lived in. The moment the phone rang he had known in his gut it was Cindy calling.

"We'll be right there. Don't let anyone near her until I arrive," he said before hanging up.

"What's going on?" Liam asked as Mark yanked open the car door.

"It's official. This is a murder investigation."

Jeremiah was in the park jogging with his dog, Captain, when he heard the first ambulance go by. It wasn't that unusual so he didn't think much of it until he heard a fire truck just a few heartbeats later. He stopped. Three police cars went by, one after the other, and that's when he knew something was really wrong.

He slipped his phone out of his pocket and tried calling Cindy. It went to voicemail. He put the phone away and headed for his car at a run with Captain racing along beside him.

Before starting the car he tried once more to get hold of Cindy. This time she picked up.

"Where are you?" he asked without preamble.

"Downtown. There's been an explosion in the bridal shop."

"Are you okay?"

"Yes, but Geanie's not."

"I'll be right there."

"The streets are jammed. They're having trouble getting the emergency vehicles through."

"I'll find a way," he assured her before hanging up.

Why was it whenever something bad happened in this town Cindy seemed to be right at the heart of it? He was less than five minutes from the store she was talking about. As he gunned the engine and ran a stop sign his mind raced on ahead to what he was going to find.

He was a little more than half a mile away from the store when he was forced to pull over to the side and park. There was a policeman up ahead turning cars around and past him Jeremiah could see a snarl of traffic.

He rolled down the window to let in air and ordered Captain to watch the car. The dog whined but sat down in the passenger seat obediently.

Jeremiah got out of the car and jogged forward.

"We're sealing off this area," the officer directing traffic told him.

"I'm a rabbi," Jeremiah responded. As a member of the clergy he had access to trauma sites that a regular civilian wouldn't necessarily have. The officer waved him through before returning his attention to the cars.

Jeremiah weaved through the parked cars, making his way toward the bridal shop. He could see smoke in the air now and his eyes were beginning to water. Cindy had said she was okay but that Geanie was not. He prayed for their safety and dreaded what he was going to find. He was supposed to be fitted for a tuxedo for the wedding in about an hour. He just hoped that it didn't end up being a black suit for a funeral instead.

Firefighters and paramedics filled the street the bridal shop was on. Jeremiah's eyes flitted everywhere. He saw Geanie's car, half covered in rubble right next to the shop, but there was no sign of Cindy. He walked a little farther and then spotted Cindy's car. There was debris on it as well, but nothing like what coated the other car.

The fire was just about out but the smoke still hung thick in the air as he jogged up to the car. Cindy was in the driver's seat, but she was looking at Geanie who was laying down on the back seat.

He rapped on the window and Cindy looked up at him startled. A moment later her door flew open and she launched herself at him, hugging him fiercely. She began to shake and he held her tight. She did seem to be alright except for a burn on her shoulder. Ash dusted her hair and clothes.

"What happened?" he asked.

"We'd like to know that, too," Mark said, walking up with his partner. He glanced at Jeremiah and shook his head. "I should be surprised that you made it here before us, but somehow I'm not."

Cindy pulled away and wiped at her eyes. "Geanie was supposed to have her new dress fitted this evening. She forgot her slip and I was bringing it to her. There was no parking so she came out here to grab it from me and then the store blew up. It knocked her unconscious and I managed to get her into the backseat. She-she hasn't woken up yet."

"Liam, get one of the paramedics over here. If he gives you any trouble, arrest him if you have to," Mark said.

Liam turned and trotted off.

"Now, what makes you think this wasn't just an accident?" Mark asked.

"Because a car tried to run us down earlier today."

"What?" Mark and Jeremiah said in chorus.

"I thought it was an accident at the time, but now..."

"Now, not so much. I get it. Why didn't you call me earlier?" Mark asked.

"We filed a police report. The clerk at the minimart where it happened got the license plate and called the police. I'm sure you can find all the information. Maybe you can find the person who did this and stop them."

"Why would someone want to kill Geanie?" Jeremiah asked.

"If you ask me, to get to Joseph," Mark said grimly.

It made sense. A man of Joseph's wealth and position was far more likely to have enemies than a graphic artist who worked for a church. That's exactly what this wedding didn't need was more drama. His secretary, Marie, had been giving him grief for weeks about being the best man at a Protestant wedding. When she heard this news, which she somehow would, she was going to be impossible to deal with.

He took a deep breath. His problems with a bossy, overprotective secretary were the least of all their worries right now. They had to figure out who was behind this and how they could keep Geanie safe.

And Cindy.

It hadn't escaped his notice that she'd also been in the line of fire for both incidents. With her as the maid of honor and the wedding right around the corner, and now all of this, she was probably going to be at Geanie's side every moment which put her in just as much danger as the bride.

Liam returned with a paramedic in tow. The man instantly began to check Geanie over. Jeremiah moved a couple of steps away and Mark followed him.

"I need to call Joseph, see if he has any clue who might want to mess up his wedding," Mark said.

"We're supposed to be having our tuxedo fittings in just a few minutes. He's probably already at the store."

Mark went pale and pulled out his phone. "What's his number?"

Jeremiah retrieved his phone and rattled off the number and watched as Mark waited impatiently for Joseph to pick up.

"Joseph, this is Detective Mark Walters. Where are you right now? Okay. Look, I need you to get out of there right now. Don't ask, just move. I'll meet you at your house in say thirty minutes. It's an emergency," Mark snapped at the end before disconnecting the call.

"You're afraid someone's going to bomb that shop, too?" Jeremiah asked.

"At the moment, anything is a possibility as far as I'm concerned. You know what they say, better safe than dead."

"What's going on?" Cindy asked.

She had gotten out of the car and was swaying slightly on her feet.

"Nothing, we were just checking up on Joseph, arranging to meet up with him," Mark said.

"Officer," the paramedic said, rising and turning toward Mark.

"Yes? How is she?"

"Well, she hit her head pretty good against something. I need to get her to the hospital. She needs to get X-rays and be thoroughly checked out."

"Fine, but you take her straight to the hospital and don't stop for anything. Cindy here will be accompanying her every step of the way. Is that clear?"

"Crystal."

"Good. Now go."

"You okay to handle this, Cindy?" Jeremiah asked.
She nodded.

"Maybe I should go, too."

"No, I need you with me and Joseph."

"Why?" Jeremiah asked.

"I just do. Do me a favor and for once just do what I tell you."

Jeremiah took a step back. "You're the detective."

"And don't forget it," Mark snapped.

Something was clearly bothering him. Maybe once they got out of here he'd be able to find out. Jeremiah glanced to the side and saw that Liam was busy taking witness statements. He wondered if Mark's partner was going to be accompanying them.

As if he'd read his mind Mark called over. "Liam!"

"Yeah?" the other cop answered.

"I need you to go the hospital with Cindy and Geanie. Don't leave them alone for a second until you hear otherwise from me."

"What's going on?"

"I'll fill you in later. Right now, you're the one I'm trusting."

Liam nodded and snapped shut his notebook and pocketed it. He moved over and stood next to Cindy even as the paramedic returned with another man and a stretcher.

They waited until they saw them all into an ambulance.

"We'll take my car," Mark said.

"Okay, but I have to get Captain first. He's waiting in my car."

"Fine, go. I'm parked just up that way," Mark said pointing.

Jeremiah nodded and headed quickly back to his car. Captain was eagerly waiting for him and a minute later he and the German Shepherd were weaving back through the cars headed for where Mark was waiting for them.

They were almost there when Captain gave a sudden, sharp tug on his leash. Jeremiah glanced down. The dog was looking off to one side, pulling in that direction.

"We're not going that way, boy," Jeremiah said, snapping his fingers to get the dog's attention.

Captain whined and turned back forward. They took two more steps and the leash went taut again. Jeremiah stopped. The dog was definitely fixated on something, although what he couldn't tell. He scanned the area, looking for something that could have set Captain off.

Suddenly he heard deep growling. He looked down. Captain had his teeth bared and all his muscles were coiled. He had never seen the dog look so menacing in the entire time he'd had him.

"What's wrong, boy?" Jeremiah asked.

The dog lunged into a small cluster of bystanders his jaws clacking together.

3

"Captain!" Jeremiah shouted as he tried to pull the dog up short. His left foot slid in something wet on the ground and he staggered, nearly falling, as he struggled to keep the dog back.

The crowd of onlookers scattered with shouts of alarm and Captain changed directions, pulling suddenly to the left. Jeremiah went down on one knee before struggling back up. He got a hand on Captain's collar and the dog swung his head toward him as if he were going to bite. He saw Jeremiah, whined, and turned away again. His claws scraped against the cement and he strained with all his might.

For one second Jeremiah thought of letting him go and following him. With this many people around, including this many police, he decided that would be a bad idea. Instead he began walking swiftly, letting Captain lead him. He finally broke into a jog. The dog continued to try to lunge forward, clearly impatient and growing more desperate.

Jeremiah heard the sound of squealing tires and looked around, but couldn't see a car leaving the area. He picked up his pace and less than a minute later Captain stopped at a spot on the next street over. He sniffed at some fresh skid marks on the ground, continuing to whine deep in his throat. He then sniffed the surrounding area before finally laying down and looking up at Jeremiah with the most wretched look on his face.

Jeremiah crouched down and inspected the skid marks as he scratched the dog behind the ears.

"Who was it, boy, who did you see?" he asked softly.

The dog laid his head down and sighed deeply. His posture reminded Jeremiah of when he had found him laying on the spot where his previous master died. Jeremiah stood slowly, wondering if it was possible that the dog had seen the man who killed his former owner. It would explain his reaction.

If that was true, though, Jeremiah had his answer. The dog's owner hadn't been killed by the same people who had been killing homeless people and stealing their dogs back then.

It took another five minutes before he could convince Captain to leave the spot. As they walked back toward where Mark would be waiting for them the dog kept looking around, but his whole manner was off.

"What kept you?" Mark asked when they finally arrived at his car.

"Captain needed a walk," Jeremiah said shortly.

"Ah, good idea. Don't need an accident in the car," Mark said, opening the back door for the dog.

Captain got in and settled down on the backseat. Once the door was closed Jeremiah got into the passenger seat.

"So, what's going on?" Jeremiah asked as Mark headed for Joseph's house.

"I got a weird note. Anonymous, of course. It was found in an envelope outside the police building today."

"What did it say?"

"It said 'Ask him what his name is.' It has to be a reference to Paul, but it makes no sense."

Jeremiah nodded. It had been just over two months since Mark had asked his and Cindy's help finding out the truth about Paul. With all the holidays, though, it had been rough to find time for anything that wasn't work related in some way.

"It certainly seems like a reference to Paul."

"It has to be. Who else could they be talking about?"

Me, Jeremiah thought. Of course, that was highly improbable.

"So, what do you make of it?"

"I don't know, he's dead, there's no way to ask him."

"And the real Paul is dead so no way to ask him either," Jeremiah said.

"So, let's review what we know. The real Paul Dryer was kidnapped at the age of eight. Two years later a ten-year-old boy claiming to be Paul was picked up wandering on the side of the road."

"But that boy was the changeling, the false Paul that grew up to be your partner."

"That's right," Mark said. "According to his younger sister, Gretchen, she was suspicious of the imposter from the first, but no one would listen to her and even though he knew almost everything about the real Paul, there were some odd gaps in his memory. She also noted that he had an aversion to church and to the word Righteousness."

"That's what she told you," Jeremiah affirmed.

"We know that at the time of his kidnapping there were supposedly a few other wealthy children kidnapped and back then police suspected a cult run by a guy named

Matthew that operated up in the hills above town, roughly where the Green Pastures camp is now located."

"Ransoms were paid but those children were never returned," Jeremiah said.

"And the police could never pin anything on the cult leader, and one day the entire cult disappeared."

"But when the one cabin was blown up at Green Pastures, dozens of bodies were discovered underneath it."

"Including one that DNA confirmed as the real Paul Dryer, kidnapped at age eight."

"Only a few of the other bodies have been identified, but no one that can be linked directly to the cult."

"However, a man named Matthew Tobias lived in the town of Righteousness where he swindled a lot of people out of money before disappearing. The timing is right for him to have reappeared here going by the name Matthew. His Wanted poster in Righteousness bore an uncanny resemblance to the Paul that you and I knew. The few people who knew Matthew Tobias in Righteousness don't recall him having a son."

"Doesn't mean he didn't. Or he could have connected with the boy afterward, kidnapped him from his mother. It seems logical that our Paul was either Matthew's son or some other blood relative, like a nephew."

"It does. The problem is proving that. Aside from that incident in Righteousness, I can't find any records for a Matthew Tobias anywhere, no marriage, birth or death records of any kind."

"So, he was a conman, that was probably an assumed name. Find his real name, or more of his aliases and you have a better chance at finding a birth certificate with his name listed as the father."

"Given that the fake Paul knew so much about the real Paul's life, it stands to reason that he either met and spent time with the kidnapped boy or-"

"Or somebody prepped him with the information as part of a more elaborate con that somehow went wrong," Jeremiah supplied.

"Exactly."

"There were no fingerprints, dental records or DNA of any kind on file for Matthew Tobias so for all we know one of those dead bodies under the cabin could be his. Or he could have died somewhere else or even be alive and well and spending his money down in South America somewhere."

"Can you try to match any of the DNA of the unclaimed bodies with our Paul's DNA?" Jeremiah asked.

Mark shook his head. "The case is officially closed and given everything that's happened it could cost me my job. Plus, I'm pretty sure the Dryer family has gone to some lengths to put this whole thing to rest. When I spoke to them, only the daughter was willing to believe that it was even possible that the boy who showed up two years after the kidnapping was not their son."

"Have you tried running down families of the other kidnapping victims?"

"No, but that's not a bad idea. Not sure if they could tell me anything, but it's worth a try."

They started up the hill leading to Joseph's mansion, and Jeremiah switched topics. "You think someone is really after Geanie?"

"I don't know, but I don't like it. Coincidences don't happen around Cindy. You either for that matter."

Jeremiah didn't say anything. He had been thinking nearly the same thing. He had grown a little paranoid about Cindy's safety, but not without good reason.

A couple minutes later they were pulling up outside Joseph's mansion. He met them at the door and escorted them in, his face scrunched up in concern. Captain came in as well and began to wag his tail when he was greeted by one of Joseph's poodles. The two headed off together while Joseph escorted Mark and Jeremiah to the living room. As soon as they were all seated, Joseph leaned forward.

"Okay, what's happened?" he asked. "It has to be important or you could have just met me at the tux shop."

"There's been an accident. Geanie was knocked unconscious and she's been taken to the hospital," Mark said.

Joseph leaped up from his seat. "Why didn't you say so? Let's get to the hospital."

Mark held up his hand. "There'll be time to see her after the doctors check her over. For now, there are more urgent concerns."

"What can be more urgent?" Joseph demanded, eyes wide.

"There's some concern that maybe what happened to her wasn't an accident."

Joseph blinked slowly and then sank back down onto his chair. "What do you mean?"

Jeremiah still wasn't sure why he was there. Perhaps it had been just because Mark wanted to talk to him about Paul on the way over. He could tell his presence in addition to Mark's was spooking Joseph.

"It's going to be okay," he said softly.

"The bridal store she was outside of...blew up," Mark said.

"What?" Joseph asked.

"There was an explosion while she was outside getting something from Cindy's car. The explosion knocked her into the car and she hit her head. That's why she's unconscious. She didn't appear to have any other injuries, but she's been taken to the hospital to be completely checked out."

"That's awful."

Mark cleared his throat. "Earlier in the day a car attempted to run her down while she and Cindy were out."

"This is a joke, right?" Joseph asked, his face draining of all color. "A surprise bachelor party or something, just trying to get me off balance, right?"

"I'm afraid not," Jeremiah said quietly. He reached out and touched the other man's hand briefly, a gesture of support and sympathy.

Joseph seemed to collapse into the chair so that it was barely keeping him upright. "This can't be happening," he whispered. "We're getting married in ten days."

"And we're concerned that perhaps this isn't all just bad luck or coincidence. We're concerned that this has something to do with the wedding," Mark said.

"How, why?"

"That's why we're here," Jeremiah said. "We're hoping that you can help us figure that out."

Joseph nodded slowly. "I'll do whatever I can."

"Good. That's good," Mark said encouragingly. "Let's start at the top. Do you have any enemies? Anyone who might want to hurt you or Geanie?"

Joseph buried his face in his hands and his shoulders began to shake. The shock was getting to him. "No, no one. I treat everyone fairly."

"Okay, anyone who might be jealous of you or your success?"

"I...I don't know how to answer that."

"Take your time," Mark said. To Jeremiah he mouthed, "It's going to be a long night."

~

Cindy felt like time had been standing still ever since the ambulance reached the hospital. Geanie had been scurried from room to room, one test to another with her and Liam trailing behind and guarding outside when they weren't allowed in. Finally they put her in a private room and after what seemed like more endless waiting a doctor came in studying a chart.

"How is she?" Cindy asked, leaping to her feet.

"At the moment, stable. There's no obvious trauma of any sort."

"But she's still unconscious."

"Yes, and obviously that's a concern. At this point we just have to watch and wait. Hopefully she'll wake up on her own in a few hours."

"And if she doesn't?" Cindy asked.

"Then, we've got other things to discuss," the doctor said. "Hopefully, it won't come to that."

Coma. That's what he wasn't saying. Cindy felt herself panic slightly at the thought. She forced herself to take a deep breath. It was okay, Geanie was going to wake up and be just fine. There was no sense thinking about the worst case scenario yet.

"I'll check back in before the end of my shift," the doctor promised.

"Thank you," she said, forcing the words out around the lump in her throat.

The doctor left and she instantly dropped her head and began to pray.

She didn't know how much time passed, but it felt like an eternity as she alternated watching and praying. She and Liam exchanged a few words occasionally and nurses came in and out checking up on Geanie whose condition didn't seem to be changing. At one point she called Jeremiah and gave him an update so he could tell Joseph and Mark what was going on.

Cindy struggled against the feelings of anxiety that threatened to overwhelm her and she kept reiterating to herself that God was in charge and that everything was going to be okay.

"I'm going to grab us some coffee," Liam said finally.

"Thanks, sounds great." She would have preferred a soda, but at this point she would take the caffeine in whatever form she could get it.

He got up and left. No sooner had he disappeared than her phone rang. She grabbed it out of her purse and blinked at the screen.

It was Gerald Wilson. She had been trying to get hold of the investigator turned author for the last couple of weeks. He had interviewed her almost a year earlier about her experiences with the Passion Week Killer for inclusion in his latest book about myths and legends surrounding notorious crimes. He had also been working on investigating the cult that had set up camp decades earlier up in the hills above Pine Springs. He had been driven out of town by an armed intruder in his hotel room who didn't like his investigations. She had called him hoping to get more information about that and to see if he could help her figure out how Paul was connected to all of it.

"Cindy, it's good to hear from you. I was on vacation and just got back in town and got your messages. I wanted to let you know that I'm dropping a copy of the book you're in into the mail today. They just came in and they won't hit stores for another month. You know, I think this one has bestseller written all over it."

"Thanks, Gerald, I appreciate that, but I've actually been trying to get hold of you so I could pick your brain about the cult that was in this area."

"Thinking of going after their buried treasure yourself?" he asked, his voice teasing.

"No, I'm trying to run down a connection. You remember the two detectives who worked on my case, Mark and Paul?"

"How could I forget?" he asked drily. "Neither was very forthcoming when I tried to interview them."

"Well, I don't know if you knew this, but a couple of days after you left town Paul was killed."

"I hadn't realized. Was it part of that land scandal mystery you were involved in?"

"Yes."

"Well, what can I help you with?"

She took a deep breath. "It turns out Paul had been lying since he was a kid about his identity. They found the body of the real Paul during that whole mess."

He whistled low.

"I've been trying to help figure out who he might have actually been and I have reason to believe he's connected to that cult."

There was a long pause on the other end and she began to wonder if the connection had been lost.

"Hello, are you still there?" she finally asked.

"Yes. Look, Cindy, there's something I should tell you."

"What?"

"Remember that I left town after an armed gunman threatened me?"

"Yes."

"I told you then I didn't care about figuring out who the man was."

"I remember."

"Well, that wasn't entirely true. I knew who threatened me because I recognized his voice."

"Who?" she asked, gripping the phone tighter. "Who threatened you because of your investigation?"

"It was Paul."

4

"Are you sure?" Cindy asked breathlessly.

"Positive. I never forget a voice."

"And you think he threatened you because of what he was afraid you might find if you kept investigating the cult?"

"With what you've just told me I'm positive that's the case."

Geanie groaned and Cindy jumped in her chair. Relief flooded her as she saw that the other woman's eyelids were fluttering. She was waking up.

"We need to compare notes," she said to Gerald.

"I'm free now."

"Unfortunately, I'm not. I have to take care of something. When can I call you?"

"I'll be home for the next three days doing nothing in particular, feel free to call whenever you can."

"Thank you," she said before hanging up and turning her attention to Geanie.

"Wh-what happened?" Geanie asked.

"You hit your head," Cindy said, not wanting to reveal too much too quickly lest she send her into shock.

Liam entered at that moment carrying two cups of coffee. Cindy took one and sipped it, wrinkling her nose at the bitterness.

"You're awake," Liam said cheerfully.

In her mind Cindy couldn't help but contrast him with Mark's former partner. Paul had always been quiet and staunchly against civilian involvement in police matters. Liam was much more friendly and easy going. At that moment, though, she couldn't help but wonder if he was hiding secrets, too.

"Yeah," Geanie said, edging herself up to more of a sitting position in the bed. "Why am I in the hospital?"

"The paramedics wanted to check you out and make sure there wasn't any brain damage."

"At least not any more than there already was?" Geanie asked wanly.

Her sense of humor seemed to be intact. That was a good sign.

"Well, you know, there was some concern in that regard, but I was able to set the doctors straight," Cindy said with a smile.

Geanie smiled back. Color was starting to return to her cheeks and she was growing more alert by the second. Cindy sent a grateful prayer heavenwards. Everything was going to be okay.

A nurse entered. "Glad to see you're awake," the woman said briskly. "That was a nasty bump on the head."

"Yeah, I'm fine, I think. When can I get out of here?" Geanie asked.

"That will be up to the doctor, but there's no way you're getting out of here tonight if that's what you're thinking," the woman said.

"But, I'm getting married in a week and a half. I've got stuff I have to do."

"And that stuff will just have to wait for you. I'll get the doctor, though. He'll want to check you over."

The doctor came in a minute later and Cindy stepped out into the hallway. She called Joseph who answered, voice tense.

"She woke up. It looks like she's going to be just fine," Cindy reassured him.

"Thank you, God," Joseph whispered. "And thank you for being there with her and for calling, and letting me know."

"Of course. It's the least I could do," Cindy said.

"Can I talk to her?"

"In a few minutes. The doctor's checking her over again now that she's awake. Hopefully he'll release her in the morning."

"Whatever they need to do, make sure they do it."

"I will."

"Okay. Call me the minute I can talk to her."

"I will," she promised before ending the call.

Poor Joseph. He had been through so much. She remembered when he had told her he was thinking of proposing to Geanie but he had been afraid to because he felt that danger had been stalking him because of all the things that had happened. Cindy had reassured him that if anyone was cursed it was her and not him.

If it was someone coming after Geanie trying to get at him then maybe all his fears had been justified. She couldn't let herself think like that, though. She couldn't let him think like it either. For all they knew at this point it really could be coincidence. Or maybe someone had a grudge against the bridal shop and Geanie just happened to get in the way.

She wanted to call Mark and find out if the police knew anything yet about the driver of the car that had nearly hit them. She knew he and Jeremiah were with Joseph, though, so it would be best just to let them get their business done.

A minute later the doctor stepped into the hallway. "We're going to keep her overnight for observation. At this point, though, I don't see any reason why we can't release her in the morning."

"That's good news, thank you."

He shrugged. "We'll see what the morning brings."

He left and Cindy went back into the room just as Liam was stepping out. "I'm going to call Mark and see if he wants to post officers outside the door tonight," he told her.

She nodded. She had a feeling the answer was going to be 'yes' unless the detective had learned something new.

"They won't let me leave until the morning," Geanie said, looking distressed as Cindy walked up to her.

"So I heard. It's a good thing, though. You need the rest and they can keep an eye on you and make sure you're okay."

"I'm fine. I don't see what all the fuss is about. How did I hit my head anyway?"

"What do you remember?"

"I came out of the shop to get the slip from you. I was at the car and there was some kind of noise and then I woke up here."

Cindy picked up Geanie's hand. "There was an explosion in the bridal shop. It threw you against the car. I think that's when you hit your head."

"An explosion?" Geanie asked, turning pale. "What kind?"

"I don't know what set it off."

"It had to be big to knock me into the car."

"Very big."

Geanie blinked. "The owner and the seamstress?"

Cindy shook her head. "There's no way they could have survived the blast."

Geanie stared at her for a moment in shock and then began to cry. Cindy wrapped her arms around her and held her close.

"I never liked either of them," Geanie sobbed after a moment.

"I know, neither did I," Cindy confessed through tears of her own.

"But I never would have wished them dead."

"Me either," Cindy said, hugging her tighter.

"If it hadn't been for forgetting my slip, and you not being able to get parking, I would be dead, too."

"I believe that God has a plan for each of us. It wasn't your time and He was going to do whatever He needed to make sure you weren't in that store when it happened."

When they had both stopped crying Cindy handed her phone to Geanie. "Joseph wanted to talk as soon as you were able."

Geanie took the phone gratefully and Cindy walked back outside where she joined Liam in the hallway.

"Figured you ladies could use some privacy," he said sheepishly.

She smiled gratefully. "So, what did Mark say?"

"He's called for an overnight protective watch, handpicked the men. As soon as the first shift gets here we're free to leave."

Cindy nodded, realizing just how tired she was.

"He also said that once she's released in the morning he wants her staying at Joseph's because of his enhanced security system."

"She's not going to like that," Cindy warned. "She's got a lot left to do for the wedding and some things she's trying to keep as a surprise from Joseph. Plus, if it gets out she's staying there I'm sure tongues will wag."

"Not if members of the bridal party are staying there, too," Liam said.

"What do you mean?"

"I mean, Mark suggested that you and Jeremiah should stay there as well plus whoever else is closely involved."

Cindy raised an eyebrow. "Then I guess when I get home I have to skip passing out in favor of packing."

Liam shrugged. "I think Mark wants everyone where he can keep close tabs on them, just in case."

"Of course, that also makes the whole bridal party one big target," she muttered.

"If it turns out this is an attack against her and Joseph, Mark's going to order round the clock security as well."

Cindy couldn't help but smile. "Okay, Royal Wedding it is."

~

Jeremiah was at home just about finished with his packing when Cindy called. "Hey, long day," he said. "How are you holding up?"

"Probably better than can be expected," she said. "You?"

"Irritated. Trying to figure out what I'm missing that I need to take to Joseph's."

"Yeah, me, too."

There was a hesitation in her voice that gave him pause. There was something she wasn't saying.

"What's wrong?"

"I have to admit, I'm feeling a bit jumpy being here by myself. They're not releasing Geanie until the morning."

"Maybe you should head on over to Joseph's tonight," he suggested. "It would be safer."

"I don't know," she said.

For some reason she was struggling with the decision although he wasn't sure why. He sighed and went to his dresser to add another pair of socks to his bag. "Tell you what, how about I pick you up in half an hour and we both head over there?"

"Really?" she said, sounding tremendously relieved.

"Sure," he said. "After all, Captain's still over there. I figured he'd just get in the way of the packing and he was having fun with Joseph's dogs. He'll miss me if I'm not there tonight, though."

He didn't want to have to go over early, but clearly Cindy needed him to do this. That was fine.

"Okay. I've got a lot of stuff, though. I'm having to pack for both of us over here."

"All the more reason you need help hauling it," he said, putting a smile into his voice.

"Thank you. I'll see you soon."

"Okay, bye."

He ended the call and zipped up his suitcase. He'd said he'd go over in half an hour, but he'd head over now. He was ready and there was no reason to leave her alone and feeling jumpy any longer than he had to.

He locked up the house, threw his bag in the trunk and headed out. Back in November he had been ready to leave because the relationship with Cindy was growing too close which was dangerous for both of them. Then Mark had begged for their help finding out the truth about Paul. He had reluctantly agreed, telling himself that once they found out the truth he would go.

Maybe that was why he hadn't worked very hard to actually help out with that. He knew he didn't want to go, but staying was becoming less of an option. Staying meant telling Cindy the truth and that was something he couldn't bring himself to do. It would shatter her. He'd spent the last couple of months trying to distance himself from her, but that hadn't worked either. Somehow they seemed to be closer than ever. Wedding planning had thrown them even more and more together and for the next ten days they would be nearly inseparable. The thought gave him a deep sense of joy while at the same time it frustrated the logical side of him that knew that much togetherness was a mistake.

Five minutes later Cindy was opening the door. She threw her arms around him and hugged him so tightly he thought she might never let go. She finally did, and he followed her into her house.

There was a massive pile of luggage next to the door and he felt his eyes bulge as he stared at it.

"I warned you there was a lot," she said.

"Yes, you did," he conceded.

"To be honest, I've run out of suitcases and I've had to resort to a couple of boxes and a trash bag. Not exactly dignified or up to the standards of a Royal Wedding."

He chuckled. "I'm sure Joseph has a few loose diamonds you can glue on them that will class them up in no time."

She stared at him for a moment and then burst out laughing so hard she sat down on the floor. After a moment he started laughing, too.

"It will be the world's first million dollar trash bag," he said.

"I'd pay to see that," she gasped. "Not a million dollars, but I'd still pay."

"And then Geanie's mother will demand to know how come the trash bag is wearing more diamonds than her daughter."

"Stop, please," Cindy said, clutching her side. "It hurts to laugh."

And just like that she had lifted his dark mood and destroyed his resolve to keep his distance. That was the magic of Cindy. It was also the danger.

"Okay, how about I start hauling some of this stuff out to the car?"

"That's a good idea," she said, slowly getting up from the floor. "I've only got a few more things to pack...I hope."

"You know there will be something Geanie will have to come back here for," he said.

"That's what I'm afraid of, and trying so hard to avoid. Oh!" she said, suddenly startled. She darted into the dining room and returned with an enormous box. "I nearly forgot the supplies for the wedding favors. We were supposed to assemble these tonight. I don't know when we're going to have time now, but it's got to be done."

"Is that all of it?" Jeremiah asked.

"No, there's five more boxes like this and then two giant boxes."

"That's a lot of wedding favors."

"Have you seen the size of the guest list?" she asked.

"I confess I haven't."

"I have. I had to go with Geanie to the post office the day she mailed out all the invitations. All fifteen hundred of them."

He stared, amazed. "And presumably a lot of those were going to homes with more than one person."

"Yup."

"So, how many people RSVPd to say they were coming?"

"So far? All of them."

"That's not possible."

"That's what Geanie said after the first two hundred all came back yes."

"For the first time I understand people who choose to elope," he said with a shake of his head.

"I know, right?" Cindy said as she went to get another box.

~

It turned out to be the world's biggest puzzle trying to fit everything into Jeremiah's car so they wouldn't have to make more than one trip. Jeremiah finally accomplished it even though it meant Cindy had to carry one of the larger boxes on her lap. The box was so large she couldn't see over it or around it and by the time they made it to Joseph's she was a bit carsick.

Joseph opened her door and took the box from her. "I thought Geanie wasn't moving all of her stuff here until after the honeymoon," he said, sounding bewildered.

Cindy got out of the car and took a deep breath of the cold air which made her feel better. "Dear, sweet, delusional Joseph. It's going to take an army to move that stuff. This is just the wedding stuff. And no peeking at any of it or she'll have my hide."

"She's serious about that," Jeremiah said as he got out of the car and popped the trunk.

"Understood. So, let's find a place where we can put all of this."

It took about an hour but they finally got everything sorted into the appropriate rooms. Cindy and Geanie were sharing guest rooms next to each other while Jeremiah was in a room across the hall. A formal sitting room Joseph never used became the repository for the boxes of wedding favor supplies and a few other things.

It was all Cindy could do not to laugh when Joseph was carrying the trash bag into the house. Jeremiah didn't help by miming putting little sparkling diamonds on the bag. Fortunately Joseph was too distracted to notice.

When everything was done Cindy stood in the sitting room surveying the boxes. She and Geanie were going to have to work on assembling the favors tomorrow, but they were running out of time and she wasn't sure how much Geanie would actually be able to do. It was time to call in reinforcements, even if they didn't want to help.

Neither Melissa nor Veronica wanted to help assemble all the favors and were pretty blunt about it on the phone

45

when Cindy called each of them. She in turn was blunt with them and gave them a raking over the coals for abandoning Geanie in her hour of need and disgracing the name "bridesmaid". In the end she had guilted both of them into promising to be there the next day to help.

With that taken care of she said goodnight to the guys, went to her room, and promptly fell asleep.

~

Cindy waited in Geanie's hospital room the next morning and found herself chafing at the delay as much as the other woman was. It was ten o'clock and she still hadn't been released. Cindy felt a bit guilty thinking of how she should have just gone in to work and waited for the call. For that matter, Joseph could have picked Geanie up.

Finally she called Sylvia. "Geanie hasn't been released yet. I'm not going to be there before lunch at this rate."

"You know what? Don't worry about it. I had a feeling something like this was going to happen. I got Dave to draft one of the high school girls into helping design and print Sunday's bulletin. He's covering the phones for you and seems to be enjoying himself a little too much. I think people keep thinking it's April Fools around here. Monday is Martin Luther King Day and the office is closed so why don't you just take the rest of today and tomorrow?"

"Are you sure? I don't know how much sick time I have left."

"Don't worry about it. The Royal Wedding needs you. We've got things more than covered here."

"I feel bad-"

"Look, you're taking care of another staff member and a church member who just happens to be our biggest financial supporter. As far as I'm concerned this is work adjacent. Besides, talking to grownups for a while is good for Dave. He forgets how you know."

"Thank you," Cindy said.

Half an hour later they finally released Geanie. Once they were in the car and on their way she launched into a laundry list of the things that had to be done. She ended with "I don't know how we're going to get all those favors assembled."

"Don't worry," Cindy said. "Melissa and Veronica will be over today after work to help with all of that."

Geanie leaned her head back with a sigh. "I don't know how you pulled that off but I have five words for you. Best. Maid. Of. Honor. Ever."

"I'll take it," Cindy said with a grin.

~

Mark's day had not been nearly as productive as he would have liked. The car that had nearly run down Geanie and Cindy the day before turned out to have been stolen before the incident. He wasn't sure if that made it more or less likely that they were being targeted. It was possible the driver had just spooked and they happened to be at the wrong place at the wrong time.

The thief had abandoned the car a few blocks from the minimart and had left behind no fingerprints to help them. Bomb squad and arson investigation officers were still going over the scene at the bridal shop to determine the cause of the explosion. Unfortunately, the bodies of the two

47

ladies who had been helping Geanie had been recovered inside.

All-in-all he felt like nothing was accomplished by the time five o'clock rolled around. With nothing left to do but wait for some word on the cause of the explosion he called Traci and let her know he'd be home on time for once. She sounded thrilled and he had a flash of guilt. There'd been a lot of late nights lately.

As he drove home his thoughts returned to Paul and the mysterious note he'd received the day before. He had forensics testing the note and the envelope but he didn't anticipate that they would actually find anything.

When he finally pulled up outside the house he shook himself mentally. He needed to learn to leave this kind of stuff at work. His wife deserved more of his undivided attention than she'd gotten in a long time.

He was halfway to the front door when it opened and Traci emerged, locking it behind her. She was wearing a long, red dress that he hadn't seen her wear in a long time. It hugged her curves in a very attention-getting way.

Traci looked beautiful, more beautiful than he could ever remember seeing her, and he stared, transfixed. She smiled at him and he was reminded again of how much he didn't deserve her.

"What's the occasion?" he finally managed to stammer. He knew it wasn't a birthday or anniversary.

"It isn't everyday my husband's actually home for dinner," she said, smiling slyly. "I thought we'd celebrate."

"I can't argue with that," he said.

"Nor should you even try."

They got into the car and he glanced at her again. "So, where are we going?"

"Rue de Main."

He whistled. It was a French restaurant and one of the nicest places in town. When Traci wanted to celebrate something, she went all out.

Twenty minutes later they were being seated at a table for two that was adorned with a white tablecloth and candles. After they had ordered their food Mark picked up her hand and kissed the back of it.

"Now, how about you tell me what's really going on Mrs. Walters?"

"Always the detective, aren't you?" she teased.

"Always."

"Okay, Mr. Detective. Why are we here?"

He blinked, taken slightly aback by her challenge. He stared at her and she simply smiled at him and cocked her head to the side as if she was waiting.

"Okay," he said at last. "Let's see. It's not already a special occasion so that implies that you have something you want to talk about, something more than just normal day-to-day stuff."

"And what might that be?" she asked.

"You wouldn't be smiling this much or have taken me someplace this nice if you were planning on leaving me."

"Very good."

"You're also smiling too much for this to be bad news which implies that whatever you want to discuss has to be important, but not bad. In fact, given how much you're smiling, you're excited about this news."

She didn't say anything, but her eyes sparkled as she looked at him.

"The choice of a romantic restaurant is symbolic. This can't be news like someone's coming for a visit. It can't be job related either. I'd say you were planning on springing a surprise vacation to Paris on me, but you would have done that at Christmas or waited for Valentine's Day. No, whatever this is, you didn't know at Christmas and it can't wait to be told until Valentine's Day, the obvious, romantic choice."

Suddenly the truth hit him so hard he actually froze, unable to speak. He stared at her, barely breathing.

"I think you just figured it out," she said softly.

"You mean?"

"Yes, Mark. We're going to have a baby."

5

At six o'clock on the dot Melissa and Veronica both showed up as promised. Melissa, a tall strawberry-blonde who looked like she'd stepped out of the pages of a magazine Cindy had met once before. She was part of a theater group that Geanie occasionally did volunteer work for. She was an aspiring actress and to Cindy's way of thinking was one of the snootiest people she'd ever met.

Veronica, on the other hand, was a complete Goth. Geanie was wild, eccentric, with crazy taste in clothing and occasionally leaned toward the Goth look, but Veronica was the whole package. Her face was pale, her hair black to match her nail polish. She was wearing a long, black velvet skirt and a black leather bustier. She had multiple ear piercings and even a nose ring. Cindy knew that Veronica and Geanie had been college roommates, but she had never actually met her.

"So, you're the new roommate," Veronica said slowly, as though it would kill her to speak at a normal pace.

"And you're the old one," Cindy said, cringing and hoping that it hadn't come out sounding catty.

If it had Veronica either didn't notice or didn't mind. She lifted her eyes and looked around. "Wow, this place is killer. Throw up some cobwebs, a coffin in the basement, and you'd have a fit lair for Dracula."

"What do you think we plan to do for next Halloween?" Geanie asked brightly as she hugged Veronica. Veronica clearly wasn't the hugging type but she seemed to tolerate it alright.

"One day, I'm going to have a place like this. Only bigger," Melissa said.

Cindy was taken aback. It was quite possibly one of the rudest things the other girl could have said.

"Good luck with that," Geanie said, her voice teasing as she hugged Veronica.

Cindy bit her tongue before she could say something snide. It was not her place to defend Geanie, or Joseph, or his house. It wasn't her place to judge Geanie's choice of bridesmaids either.

"Let's adjourn to the study where we've got some work to do," she said instead. "Joseph was kind enough to have Togo's send some deli platters."

Togo's was by far the best sandwich shop in the area and Cindy had been thrilled with Joseph's choice. She'd been even more thrilled with the fact that he'd come up with the idea on his own. She'd always known the man had great taste. After all, he was marrying Geanie.

"You're the one that keeps finding dead bodies, aren't you?" Veronica asked as Cindy lead the way to the study.

"Yeah, that would be me," Cindy said, taken aback by the question.

"That must be so...killer."

"It's downright terrible, a nightmare, in fact," Cindy said. "I wouldn't wish the experience on anyone," she added fervently.

"Chill. I'm just trying to put the name with the face. And I think it's cool that you like solve mysteries and stuff."

Cindy took a deep breath, regretting the fact that she'd strong-armed both women into coming over to help. She was starting to think she would have been a lot happier not having to deal with either of them until the bachelorette party.

"Thanks. I will admit that solving puzzles and riddles can be...exciting." She hated to admit it, especially to Veronica, but it was true. Suddenly she was even more eager to get Gerald called back as she thought about it. Even though she had a lot to deal with in the here and now, solving the mystery of Paul was going to be satisfying, especially since there was no way it could get her killed.

They made it into the study. The deli platters were set up on one table. There were some mini sandwiches along with cold cuts and fresh bread to build their own. There was also a couple dozen cans of soda chilling in a large cooler and a tray of chocolate chip cookies and brownies.

"I've made a sign for the occasion," Geanie said with a smirk. She showed it to them. It read No Boys Allowed.

Cindy laughed. "Well, that's rather specific."

"Just wanted to make sure everyone was clear on this point," Geanie said with a laugh. She affixed it to the outside of the heavy wooden door before closing it. "There, now we won't be disturbed and we can work in freedom and peace."

They loaded up paper plates with food and sat down on the plush velvet couches to eat.

"I could get used to this," Veronica said at one point, stroking the red velvet.

"Very old school. Classic. I like it," Melissa said.

"I just think it's comfy," Geanie said around a mouthful of salami and cheese sandwich.

"And just think, in a few days, this will all be yours," Veronica said.

"Must be nice to marry rich," Melissa joked.

Cindy cringed inwardly as Geanie went completely still. She finished chewing and then very carefully said, "I would love Joseph and marry him even if he didn't have a cent to his name."

"Sure you would, but all this can't hurt," Veronica said.

Geanie turned pale. That was her angry look and Cindy was doubly regretting setting up this evening. "All of this," Geanie said, waving her hand around the room, "doesn't matter. It's about how a man treats you, who he is as a person, what's in his heart. Joseph loves me, he loves God, and he is the most compassionate, witty man I have ever met. I would fight for him and he for me. I always know exactly where I stand with him and I always know I can trust him. Love is about mutual respect and admiration, commitment, friendship, and a meeting of the heart, mind, and soul. It has nothing to do with stuff."

It was beautifully and eloquently put and Cindy surreptitiously wiped a tear from her eye. She knew there had been some people who had given Geanie crap, intimated the same thing her so-called friends just had. But Cindy had seen the relationship between Geanie and Joseph from the very beginning and she knew that what the two of them had was real and special. It was the kind of relationship that every woman should strive for.

"Sorry," Veronica muttered.

"Yeah," Melissa said.

Cindy doubted very much whether either of them were sincere, but Geanie seemed more than willing to let it go. The other woman took a deep breath. Color returned to her cheeks and she picked her sandwich back up.

"Besides, Joseph is smoking hot," she said.

They all laughed at that and just like that the tension was broken for which Cindy was immeasurably grateful.

"I do have to say," she commented as she picked up her own sandwich, "that if you guys ever do any remodeling, I have dibs on these couches."

"No fair!" Veronica and Melissa echoed in chorus. That just led to more laughter and they chatted about the wedding and guys as they finished eating.

When they were all stuffed and lounging on the couches Melissa finally spoke up. "Okay, so what are these wedding favors and what do we have to do with them?"

"So glad you asked," Geanie said, perking up. "There is some assembly required, obviously, and there are...quite a number of them."

She stood up and led the way over to the massive table that housed the supplies. Geanie opened one of the smaller boxes and then one of the larger boxes and began to pull things out.

"You have got to be kidding me!" Veronica said, eyes bulging.

"That is certainly...unique," Melissa said, clearly struggling for words.

Cindy smirked at the other women's reactions. She, too, had been surprised when Geanie first laid out her idea to her. Fortunately now she could just look cool and calm in front of the others.

"Perfect, aren't they?" Geanie gushed.

Melissa shook her head. "You really are taking this wedding to a whole other level. I don't think in my wildest dreams I could ever come up with something like this."

"It's you, very you," Veronica said with a shake of her head. She looked admiringly at Geanie.

"And the best part?" Geanie said. "Joseph has no idea."

"Wow. How long do you think you're going to be able to keep it a surprise?" Melissa asked.

"All the way until we get to the reception. I'm going to need some help getting all these placed when we set up the reception area."

"At least that will probably take less time than it's going to take to put all this together," Melissa said.

"Don't count on it," Cindy said with a smirk. "You haven't seen her plans for the table layouts."

"What have we gotten ourselves into?" Veronica asked.

"A wedding. A glorious, perfect wedding and the only one I will ever have," Geanie said with a glowing smile.

Seeing the joy on her face made Cindy's own heart flood with warmth. She was so happy for her and she was growing more excited to see how this whole wedding was going to come off.

"Royal Wedding," Cindy said.

"Isn't it just," Melissa agreed, with the slightest twinge of jealousy in her voice.

Cindy couldn't blame her. Underneath all the joy and love and pride, she was feeling a bit of that herself.

~

It was midnight and Mark couldn't sleep. He kept glancing over at Traci who was sleeping peacefully, an angelic smile on her face. They were having a baby. The reality of that was still sinking in. Even still he marveled at all the changes that just that knowledge was bringing about.

He had always been protective of Traci but now he felt like he wanted to put her in a bubble where nothing could ever touch her let alone harm her. Something told him it was going to be even more intense when the baby arrived. He had to do everything in his power to protect them. Be eternally vigilant. Stop making stupid choices that could endanger any of them.

He sighed and flipped over on his side, wishing for a brief moment that he was religious. He would have appreciated being able to talk through and sort out the complicated feelings he was having with some supreme being who cared and listened. Perhaps for the first time in his life he truly understood those who embraced religion. He had always respected people like Cindy and Jeremiah, but deep down he'd never gotten it, thinking of religion as a crutch for those who needed it.

Now he realized he would give just about anything for something like that. He thought back over the past year and wondered how things might have been different if he had believed in something other than himself.

One thing Cindy and Jeremiah had done for him was to help open his eyes and show him just how complex faith and a relationship with God could be. Jeremiah killed bad people, Mark knew that. Until meeting Jeremiah he wouldn't have thought someone like him could do that and then go right back to the synagogue and carry on with his rabbinical duties.

Cindy lived her faith as a real, living, breathing part of her life. It wasn't just being in church on Sundays, singing some songs and reciting some prayers. She acted as though God played an active, integral part in her life. She was the walking epitome of the whole "work like everything depends on you and pray like everything depends on God" thing. He believed absolutely that her faith had gotten her through situations that would have made other people crumble. He also wondered sometimes if she lived a seemingly charmed life, escaping death repeatedly, because of her relationship with God. Maybe God wanted Cindy alive and therefore nothing could touch her.

It was a lot to think about. Now that he was going to be a father and responsible for a tiny life he couldn't help but think about it though. Maybe the meaning of life was realizing that you were responsible not just to someone else but for someone else.

That was him. A father-to-be. Responsible. He needed to start acting like it.

He got up and Buster lifted his head from where he was laying on the foot of the bed. The beagle wagged his tail twice before dropping his head back down. It seemed Mark was the only one having trouble sleeping.

He paced out into the living room, trying to clear his head. There was just so much to think about and so much to do. They were going to need to set up a nursery. Bye-bye guest room. Not that anyone visited much. Occasionally one of Traci's relatives would come to visit. Although with her sister getting more and more involved with the coven she had joined she came around a lot less than she used to. He knew Traci was worried about her and felt like her sister was changing, slipping away from her.

It happened in families all the time. Maybe not as dramatically, but still. He took a deep breath and vowed that he'd never let that happen with their child. They would always be close.

His own father hadn't been the warmest of men and Mark was determined to break that cycle. He wanted to be there for his kid, go to soccer games or ballet recitals or whatever it was they were into. He wanted to laugh and play together, take them to their first baseball game.

A lump formed in his throat. The first baseball game of the season had been a tradition with him and Paul. Paul was gone. Time to start a new tradition.

Time to do a lot of things different.

He sat down on the couch but didn't turn on the television, not wanting to wake Traci. She was sleeping for two and he wanted her to get as much rest as she needed. He dropped his head into his hands and struggled to quiet his mind, wanting to just be able to relax enough so he could go back to bed and get some sleep.

He had just about achieved some semblance of calm when he heard his phone vibrating on the kitchen counter. He'd been so distracted he'd forgotten to take it into the bedroom earlier. He got up and went to retrieve it. It was dispatch calling.

"Mark here," he said quietly.

"You wanted to be alerted if there was any sign of trouble up at the Coulter residence."

"Yes, and?" Mark asked, tensing up instantly.

"The alarm system was tripped about three minutes ago."

"Has the owner called in?"

"No. We're trying to reach him."

"Alright, send squad cars."

"Already done."

"Good. I'm on my way."

He hung up and nearly dashed outside in his pajamas. He gritted his teeth and scurried back into the bedroom trying to grab clothes silently in the dark. He didn't want to wake Traci, especially since she'd ask what was going on and he'd have to admit there was trouble at Joseph's. He didn't want her worrying.

He finally managed to grab what he needed and he dressed hurriedly in the living room before grabbing his phone, gun, badge and keys and dashing out the door.

~

Cindy was restless. She tried to attribute it to sleeping in a bed that wasn't hers, but it was more than that. Besides, she'd slept fine in this bed the night before. Of course, passed out was more akin to what had happened, she had been so exhausted.

Finally she got up. She threw on a cushy white robe that Joseph had supplied and which was hanging in her closet. Staying at his home was just like being at some really fancy hotel. There were slippers, too, but she was fine with just her socks.

She left her room, closing the door quietly behind her. She glanced at both Geanie and Jeremiah's rooms, but there was no light coming from under either door. So much for someone else being up that she could talk to.

Maybe Joseph was. She headed down the hall, trying to remember where his room was. She was pretty sure it wasn't located in the guest wing. She wasn't sure it was even on the same floor. Maybe she'd get lucky and find him awake and prowling around just like her.

She hadn't had a chance to call Gerald back and that was bothering her. She promised herself she would take care of that first thing in the morning. She rationalized it by telling herself that what was going on with Geanie and the potential attacks and everything to do with the wedding was more pressing than a cold case that had gone unsolved for who knew how long. It wasn't like finding the answers would bring Paul back.

Still, she did feel bad. The sooner she could find answers the sooner hopefully Mark could get some closure with the whole thing. The need for closure was something she completely understood.

She headed down the grand staircase to the first floor, hoping to catch Joseph awake and prowling around the kitchen or living area. She didn't see any lights on but the sky outside was clear and there was a full moon which was shining through the windows and providing more than enough light to find her way around.

None of the dogs appeared to be awake. Although she knew that Captain was sleeping in Jeremiah's room and she suspected that one or more of Joseph's prize poodles were in his room.

The kitchen was dark and empty and she hesitated there for a moment, thinking about making herself a sandwich. She was feeling rather hungry. Dinner had been hours before. Of course, if she could have slept like a normal person it wouldn't be an issue.

There should still be a whole bunch of cold cuts in the fridge. Her stomach grumbled at the thought. Maybe a sandwich was a good idea.

She heard the creak of a door. It wasn't very loud, and she could swear it was coming from the first floor. Maybe Joseph was awake after all.

She turned and left the kitchen, making her way to the foyer, hoping that once there she'd either see him or figure out where he'd gone.

She was nearly there when she heard a faint step, so light she thought for a moment she had imagined it. She walked out into the foyer and swiveled her head. Her eyes fell on the front door and she noticed that it was ever so slightly ajar. That made no sense.

She turned and screamed as she came face-to-face with a man in a mask.

6

Jeremiah awoke to the sound of Cindy screaming. He vaulted out of bed, yanked open his door and ran down the hall. The sound had come from far away, so it couldn't be from just across the hall. He also registered as he ran that it was a sad statement on their recent lives that he could hear a scream and know that it was hers and not Geanie's or someone else's.

He made it to the stairs and glanced down. He saw moonlight shining on Cindy's hair and he could see someone dressed all in black struggling with her, their hand clamped over her mouth.

Jeremiah vaulted the stairs, crouching to distribute the impact throughout his body as he landed so he wouldn't break anything. At the thud of his landing the man jerked toward him.

Cindy bit the hand that was covering her mouth and the man made a sharp hissing motion but did not let go. Jeremiah blinked. It took years of training, experience, not to react to something that painful.

Jeremiah coiled himself to lunge, trying to see if the man was armed before he did so. The last thing he needed was for the intruder to cut him or Cindy because he failed to see a knife.

The man seemed to have his hands full with just Cindy, though, who was writhing and thrashing. She brought her foot down on his instep and elbowed him in the stomach.

He flung her away from him so hard that she fell and slid several feet across the marble floor, and turned to face Jeremiah head-on. Jeremiah brought his hands up, and began to circle, sizing up his opponent.

The man stared at him from behind a mask. In the darkness Jeremiah couldn't make out the color of his eyes. He lifted his hands, lunged forward as if to attack, then at the last moment threw himself sideways.

He hit the door at a run and flung it open. Jeremiah chased after him. A moment later his bare feet were slapping against the asphalt of Joseph's driveway. The thief was fast and he was already on the lawn heading for the woods.

Jeremiah heard the roar of a car engine a moment before a car rounded the last bend of the road leading up the hill. High beams hit him square in the face and Jeremiah staggered to a halt.

"Police!" someone shouted.

Jeremiah pointed. "The intruder went that way!" he shouted.

He heard a car door open and the sound of running feet as one of the officers gave chase. Jeremiah knew, though, the man would be too late. He bit back a curse, struggling to bring himself under control and hide his frustration. The police had terrible timing. Thirty seconds earlier or thirty seconds later and the guy would be in either their custody or Jeremiah's.

The second officer got out of the car and approached Jeremiah cautiously. Just then Joseph, Cindy, and Geanie came out the front door. Jeremiah could hear another engine revving as someone pushed their car up the drive too fast. It sounded like there was another one just behind it, too.

Seconds later both of the other cars had parked. Two more officers had gone after the first and Mark was striding toward them, his face ashen.

"What happened here, is everyone okay?"

"Cindy startled an intruder," Jeremiah said. "I chased him out here. When your men intercepted me he got away."

Mark stepped farther forward. "Are you hurt?" he asked Cindy.

"Just shaken."

"Okay, let's move this party inside," he said.

Jeremiah took one last look out toward the forest, furious that the man had escaped, before turning and following the rest of them inside.

In the foyer Cindy recounted her experience of finding the intruder.

"And I'm guessing you heard her scream and came running?" Mark said drily as he glanced over at Jeremiah.

"Don't I always?" Jeremiah asked with a shrug.

"Samaritan," Mark muttered. It was an old joke between the two of them.

"He had grabbed Cindy and had his hand over her mouth when I...got down here," Jeremiah said, omitting the part about vaulting the staircase.

Cindy either hadn't seen that or didn't let on. "I tried to bite him, elbow him, everything. When he saw Jeremiah though he threw me onto the floor."

"I thought he was going to attack me, but instead he went out the door," Jeremiah finished.

"Did either of you notice anything in particular about him?"

"He was close to my height, but he was dressed all in black, wearing a mask, can't tell you anything else about him," Jeremiah said.

"When he had hold of me, he did say something," Cindy said, looking suddenly uneasy.

"Well, what was it?" Mark prodded.

Cindy glanced quickly at Geanie and then just as quickly away. "He said, 'tell him there won't be any happy ending'. That was it. His voice was low, raspy."

There was silence for a moment and then Geanie sat down abruptly on the stairs. She looked like she was about to cry. "Who would try to sabotage our wedding?" she sobbed after a moment.

"That's what we need to find out," Mark said grimly. "At least now we have proof that that's what's going on here. I think it's safe to rule yesterday's events as anything but accidents."

An officer came in, interrupting them.

"What is it?" Mark asked tersely.

"We discovered that the alarm system for the main house and grounds were tampered with, that's why no audible alarm sounded. It was a real slick job, too, the guy knew what he was doing. Simply cutting the alarm triggers a signal but he worked around it somehow. He took out the phone line at the same time."

"Then how did you guys know to show up?" Joseph asked, sounding bewildered.

"The independent system halfway down your hill that monitors all approaches up he missed. That triggers a silent alarm to the alarm company who called us," Mark said. "And we tried to call you, but this explains why your phone line was down. It doesn't explain, though, why you weren't picking up your cell phone. I tried calling a dozen times on my way here."

"Battery's dead," Joseph said, flushing uncomfortably. I wore it out texting Geanie after we both turned in for the night."

Mark rolled his eyes and muttered something under his breath.

"You should have called my phone," Jeremiah said quietly.

"Well, clearly I wasn't thinking straight. It's been a bit of a crazy night, you know?" Mark snapped.

Jeremiah sensed more had happened than Mark was sharing, but he didn't press. The detective would tell them what was going on in due time.

Another officer came in. "No sign of the intruder."

Jeremiah wasn't surprised but Mark looked like he was ready to kill someone. "Great, just great," the detective said, heaving an exasperated sigh.

Jeremiah held his tongue, not wanting to end up the focus of the other man's frustration. He glanced at Cindy who was staring at Geanie with a worried look on her face. He knew it had killed her to admit in front of the other woman what the assailant had said to her, but the truth had to come out sooner or later. Geanie deserved to know that she really was in danger. He could only imagine what might have happened if it had been Geanie who surprised the intruder and not Cindy. This whole night could have easily turned tragic.

Mark passed a hand in front of his face. "Okay, this is what we're going to do. We're going to regroup in the morning, put our heads together, and see if we can't figure this out. I'm hoping some sleep will help us all to think more clearly. I know I, for one, can use the rest."

"Okay," Joseph said, sitting down beside Geanie and putting his arm around her. She leaned her head against his shoulder and nodded.

"It's settled then. I'll be back here in the morning. Hopefully then we can straighten this entire mess out so we can all get on with our lives."

~

Mark stationed officers outside, roaming the grounds of the mansion even though everyone agreed that whoever had tried to break in probably wouldn't try again that night. Once they were in place and the rest of the officers had left Cindy took Mark and Jeremiah into the sitting room.

"We need to talk," she told them both.

"Is everything okay?" Jeremiah asked.

"It's fine. It's just that I have some new information about Paul," Cindy said.

"That's okay, I don't need to hear it. And you can drop the hunt, but thanks for all your help," Mark said.

"Oh, you want to pick it back up after we figure out what's going on with Geanie. That makes perfect sense. We can't afford to be distracted from that," Cindy said.

"You don't understand. I'm not sure...sure I want to pursue this anymore," Mark said.

Cindy stared at him, convinced she couldn't have heard right. "Why? This has been so important to you. And now we're getting closer. I thought the truth was all that mattered."

"Yeah, but that was before," Mark mumbled.

"Before?" Jeremiah asked sharply.

"What's happened? Has someone threatened you? Are you worried you'll find out something you wished you hadn't?" she pressed.

"No, it's nothing like that."

"Then what is it like? Before what?"

"Before I found out I was going to be a father."

There was silence for a moment as what he'd just said sunk in.

"Congratulations," Jeremiah said, the first to speak.

"Mark, Traci's pregnant? That's wonderful!" Cindy said, finding her voice.

"Yes. Wonderful. Terrifying. All of it. The point is, I've got to start being more careful, take less risks. I want to be there for my kid as he or she grows up, you know?"

"That's perfectly understandable," Jeremiah said.

Cindy took a deep breath. She knew Mark wasn't going to like what she was about to say. "That sounds good and noble and like the right thing to do, but I know you. Not knowing is going to keep eating away at you year after year and eventually it's going to be too much. I think you owe it to your child to find out the truth so you can finally have some peace, some closure, and be able to focus all your attention on them."

She braced herself, waiting for him to argue, to explode, something. Instead he just stood there quietly. She glanced at Jeremiah who just shrugged. She was right. She knew she was. Whether or not Mark was ready to deal with that was another story altogether.

"I need to think," Mark said at last, sounding very tired. He pressed his hand to his forehead as though he had a headache. "It's just...a lot...you know."

"I know," she said. "We're here for you, though," she said, reaching out and putting a hand on his shoulder. "You've always been there for us."

"Thank you," Mark said, voice shaking slightly. "Look, I need to call it a night. We'll regroup tomorrow, okay?"

"Okay," Jeremiah said softly. "Try to get some rest. I think we're all going to need it."

"I have a terrible feeling that you're right about that," Mark said.

~

As soon as Mark had left Jeremiah turned to Cindy. "Well, that was a surprise."

"It sure was," she said quietly.

"You okay?"

"Yeah, just, Mark and Traci are having a baby. That's amazing."

Jeremiah smiled. "People have babies all the time."

"I know it's just usually not the people I know. I mean, *really* know. I almost feel like I'm going to be an aunt."

He grinned at her. "You'd make a wonderful aunt."

"You think?"

"I do. I also think you'd make a wonderful mother."

As soon as the words escaped his mouth he regretted them.

Cindy looked up at him sharply and her cheeks turned red. He forced himself to smile. "Come on, let's raid Joseph's refrigerator, I'm hungry. Last one there makes the sandwiches."

"You're on," Cindy said before racing toward the kitchen.

Jeremiah ran behind her, but let her win by just a hair. She turned, laughing, her hand on the refrigerator handle.

"I'd like a roast beef with cheddar cheese."

"At least you didn't ask for ham," he said with a smile.

"Hmmm...maybe I should change my order," she teased.

"Do so at your own peril," he threatened.

"I don't know," she said, starting to pull open the refrigerator.

He grabbed her hand and held it a moment, rubbing his thumb lightly over the back of it. Her hands were soft, they always were. Impulsively he brought it to his lips and kissed the back of it before letting it go.

She stared at him in shock. "What was that for?" she asked at last.

"To distract you while I get the roast beef," he said as he yanked open the refrigerator.

It was a lame lie, but it was the best one he could come up with.

~

Cindy felt like she was up for most of the rest of the night replaying in her mind the moment where Jeremiah had kissed her hand. She had no idea what to make of it. He had never done anything like that in the past. Around five in the morning she finally convinced herself that she was reading too much into it.

She woke up a few hours later to realize that she was the last up, though not by much it seemed. Joseph was busy in the kitchen making waffles while Jeremiah and Geanie were keeping him company.

"He cooks, too? I think he's a keeper," Cindy said to Geanie.

"You know it. He *likes* to cook, can you believe that?"

"It's a guy thing. I swear more guys actually enjoy cooking than girls do."

"You might even be right about that," Joseph said.

The waffles were amazing as it happened and Cindy had hers slathered with strawberries and whipped cream.

"A girl could get used to this," she teased as she finished her last bite.

"Think of all the slumber parties we can have, and we can make Joseph cook breakfast in the morning," Geanie said.

"Now that is a plan."

"Are guys invited to these slumber parties?" Jeremiah asked with a smile.

"No!" Cindy and Geanie chorused together and then immediately started laughing.

"Wait, I can't come to the party, but I'm expected to cook for it?" Joseph said.

"You're catching on, Sweetie," Geanie said.

"I think I'm being used."

Jeremiah smiled. "Yeah, but something tells me you don't mind."

Joseph lowered his voice and leaned in closer. "I don't, but don't tell them that."

Cindy started laughing even harder. It felt good to find a moment of semi-normality amidst the chaos. Then again, normality was a hard word to apply to either Joseph or Geanie.

"Alright, I'll clean up, you kids go have fun," Geanie said after a moment.

"Best wife ever," Joseph beamed.

"Technically I don't think you're allowed to say that until *after* the wedding," Cindy said.

"You have lousy rules," Joseph said, fake pouting. "Actually, Mark called and he's not going to be over until about noon so I thought this would be a good time to take another run at the tuxedo shop."

"Okay," Jeremiah said. "Let me go grab the shoes I'll be wearing and I'm all set to go.

"I've got a couple of things to do," Cindy said.

The others nodded and she hurried back to her room where she got her phone and called Gerald.

He picked up quickly. "I wondered how long you'd be able to contain your curiosity and your thirst for knowledge," he said good-naturedly.

"Longer than I thought I was going to be able to," she admitted. "Things have been...crazy...here."

"You'll have to tell me about it."

"Some other time. Right now I want to focus on sorting out the Paul issue. So, what else can you tell me about the cult?"

"Right to business. Alright. Let's see, the cult was based in the mountains above Pine Springs on the site of an old campground. That same campground was later purchased and refitted to make Green Pastures. Thanks to the land's history the local churches were able to purchase it fairly cheaply."

"So, when was the cult there?"

"Twenty-six years ago a man named Matthew appeared seemingly from out of nowhere. He had half a dozen people with him from the accounts I've been able to dig up. He was preaching peace, that people should lay down their arms, love their neighbors, all harmless stuff on the surface. One of his tenants was that material possessions, corporate jobs, and things of that nature corrupt people and turn them from loving, innocent creatures into greedy, manipulative people."

"And I'm guessing some people bought into what he was saying."

"More than you can imagine. He actually managed to get himself a radio show if you can believe that and people came from several different states to learn from him and to join his nature-loving group. This was the late eighties. It was post-hippy and pre-environmentalist and a lot of people with those kinds of attitudes had nowhere to go. He provided not only an avenue for expression but also a place to live and food to eat."

"In exchange for all their worldly goods."

"Right. Rumor has it he had almost everything converted to gold and precious jewels which he hid somewhere on the site. He only kept enough cash to buy the supplies the group couldn't grow or make on their own. That treasure is what has sent a lot of people up into those hills hunting for remains of the cult."

"I'm guessing the locals didn't like all this in their backyard."

"Not one bit. There were some skirmishes until Matthews banned his people from going into town at all. Naturally this raised red flags for the families of those people. He started having the things they needed delivered up the mountain."

"Then, the first child went missing. Dietrich Schmidt. His family was wealthy. The F.B.I. got involved. The parents paid five million dollars for the return of their son. Whoever kidnapped him took the money but never returned the child. The authorities could never prove who was behind the kidnapping but, obviously, the cult came under suspicion because they were already a bone of contention in the community. Plus, Dietrich's cousin was one of its members so there was a theory that he could have lured the child away from the playground where he was last seen."

"That's terrible."

"Four other children were taken, with the same results. Then Paul was the last. Two years later he showed up, and we obviously have doubts that he was the same boy that was taken. What I do know is he is the only boy to have shown up, either real or imposter. Now, here's where things get interesting."

"What is it?" Cindy asked, feeling breathless.

"As it turns out, a week after Paul turned up, the cult vanished completely. No one saw signs of them leaving town, and they would have had to pass through Pine Springs on their way to anywhere else. The couple of businesses that were delivering weekly supplies up there arrived to find the place empty, no signs of anyone. What's even weirder, when authorities searched the area later that day, they couldn't find signs that the cult had ever been there."

"That is weird."

"It was as though they had never been there. There was speculation for years that they had moved farther into the mountains, but several searches revealed no evidence of that. Eventually people decided that somehow they must have snuck through town, perhaps in small groups, and moved somewhere else. I find that theory improbable for a number of reasons. One of the chief ones being that there's no evidence of the group ever surfacing somewhere else. In theory they would still need to do business with someone for the same sorts of supplies they were having ordered in before."

"The mass grave that was discovered contained the bodies of the cultists," Cindy said.

"Yes, I would agree. That in itself, though, poses some interesting questions. Who killed them, how and why? Someone had to bury the bodies which means someone survived that massacre. Was it Matthew? Did he move on to greener pastures with his now vast wealth? Or was it one of the other cultists? Or perhaps it could have even been an outsider."

A chill danced up Cindy's spine. "Is it possible that it was Paul?"

There was a pause on the other end of the line. "I'd have to check my notes, go back over my interviews and see exactly what time the last successful delivery happened. It would also be helpful to know where on the road Paul was found by the police and at what exact time."

"That would be awful," Cindy whispered.

"It's possible the boy buried them. It's possible he escaped before or during the massacre."

"Do you think it's possible that Matthew was his father?"

"I don't recall if there were stories of a boy being one of the first who arrived with Matthew. I will have to pull up those interviews. Fortunately, as you know, I record all my interviews and I also keep those."

"Please tell me when you find out more. I'll see if I can pinpoint the timing of Paul's reappearance."

"Excellent. Given that the man risked everything by threatening my life, he must have had something powerful to hide. Whoever he was, I'm willing to bet he knew full well he was not the real Paul and that he knew what happened, or what was going to happen, to those people."

"So, it's possible Paul was a killer, even though he was only ten."

"My dear, if not a killer, he might well have been an accomplice."

7

Cindy told Gerald everything she knew, including the things that Mark had discovered in Righteousness. They agreed to touch base again with each other in two days. After hanging up she just sat for a few minutes pondering what they had talked about.

There was so much going on with the wedding and whoever wanted to hurt Geanie that she really didn't have time to fixate on the Paul mystery. If anything, she should be fixated on the Geanie mystery. Sitting alone in the room, though, she admitted to herself that that mystery scared her. She didn't truly believe that there were any skeletons in either Joseph or Geanie's closets, but just admitting out loud that someone wanted to do them harm made her feel sick to her stomach.

"Ignoring it isn't going to make it go away," she said out loud. Instead, the best course of action would be to do what she could to stop it and soon so that they could all get back to enjoying the Royal Wedding.

Unfortunately, she had no idea where to start. At least she wasn't alone in this, and, hopefully, when they all put their heads together in a couple of hours things would start to make sense.

She got up and went downstairs to find that Geanie had apparently finished up in the kitchen. She moved back into the foyer and looked up the grand staircase. It really was a massive house. Searching for her could take forever. The guys were gone, though, so it should just be the two of them in the house. She knew it was incredibly undignified, but she threw back her head and shouted, "Geanie, where are you?"

She tilted her head to listen, but there was no answering call. After a few seconds fear pricked at her spine.

Calm down, there are police outside. Nothing could have happened to her in the last few minutes, she told herself.

Theorizing that maybe Geanie had gone back to her room and Cindy hadn't heard her earlier she raced back upstairs and down the hall. She knocked on Geanie's door.

"Geanie, are you in there?"

She listened, but didn't hear anything. After a minute she tried the door. It was unlocked so she opened it and went in. The room was empty. She made her way from there to the study where all the wedding favors were neatly boxed up and divided by table. There was no sign of Geanie there either. She climbed up to the third floor and looked about once she reached the landing. Joseph's mansion was sprawling and she'd never toured all of it so she had no idea where to look next.

She cupped her hands around her mouth and shouted for Geanie again. Once more only silence greeted her. Maybe Geanie had decided to go outside for some reason. She could be getting some fresh air or playing with one of the dogs. Cindy raced down the stairs and out the front door.

One of the officers guarding the house looked over from his position by the drive and waved. She jogged over to him.

"What's up?" he asked.

"Have you seen Geanie?"

"No. Why?"

"I can't find her. You're sure she didn't come out here?"

"I haven't seen her. Do you want me to help you search, call in a team?"

"No, I'm sure she's around here somewhere," Cindy said.

The truth was, if they needed to call in a search team they probably weren't going to like what they found. She had to believe Geanie was somewhere in the house. The question was, why wasn't she answering? Had she not heard her calling? It was possible. She could be listening to music. Or maybe she was just really needing some alone time.

"Thanks anyway," she told the officer.

Cindy marched back to the house, determined to open every single door until she found her. Once she was back inside she pulled her cell phone out of her pocket and tried calling Geanie, but it just went to voicemail. She turned and headed to the right, trying to remember what was in that direction in the house.

She caught a splash of color out of the corner of her eye, and she stopped and turned. There was Geanie, standing stock still, next to a small table positioned underneath the grand staircase, invisible from the foyer. She was staring at something in her hand that Cindy couldn't quite see from the angle she was approaching.

Something in Geanie's posture, coupled with the fact that she hadn't responded to her calling, frightened Cindy more than words could say.

"What is it?" Cindy asked, approaching hesitantly.

"It seems to be a message," Geanie said, her voice strained. She looked up at Cindy with fear-filled eyes.

She was holding a black rose stripped of leaves with a card attached to it.

Cindy licked her lips. "Where did you get that?"

"I found it here, on this table back here. You know, in the old days, tables like this were used for people to leave their calling cards."

"Also in the old days people used flowers to convey intricate messages," Cindy said.

"That's right," Geanie said with a nod. "The language of flowers."

There was no need to ask what a black rose meant, the meaning was pretty self-explanatory. "What does the card say?" Cindy asked.

"It says 'No happy endings.'"

Cindy took a deep breath. That's what the intruder had told her the night before. He had also been behind her when she'd been staring at the front door. He must have left the rose on the table before she surprised him.

"What does he want from us?" Geanie asked, her voice quavering.

Cindy walked forward and took the rose from Geanie, careful not to prick herself on one of the thorns. She stared at it for a moment before setting it back down on the table.

"I don't know, but we're going to find out."

"He keeps saying 'no happy endings'."

"Well, that's where he's wrong. There is a happy ending for you and for Joseph. Happily ever after, just like in a fairy tale."

"How do you know?"

"Because I just do," Cindy said, putting as much conviction into the words as she could. "When Mark gets here we'll show this to him. Maybe it's just the clue he needs to run this guy down."

"You think so?" Geanie asked.

No, she didn't, but she wasn't about to say that to Geanie. "Absolutely. This guy has slipped up and we're going to catch him and put him away forever. The only one who won't be getting a happy ending is him. Why, I bet by tonight he's behind bars."

She put her arm around Geanie and steered her toward the kitchen. Some hot tea might be good for both of them.

"I hope so," Geanie breathed. "All my family arrives tomorrow and I don't know what I'll do if this is still going on."

Cindy winced having forgotten about Geanie's parents and her cousin. She believed there were some other relatives, too, but they were staying at a hotel. Her parents and cousin had been supposed to stay with them at their house. Which meant that now they'd be staying here, too. Right in the line of fire along with the rest of them.

Cindy was on the verge of suggesting that maybe they should send them to a hotel, too, but quickly changed her mind. Geanie was exhibiting some classic symptoms of shock and she didn't need to be trying to make a decision like that at the moment. When the guys got back and Mark arrived then she could bring it up and they'd all decide together what to do. In this case five heads were certainly better than two.

~

Mark was feeling more than a little unsettled as he stared at the reports in his hand. The stolen car that had nearly run down Geanie and Cindy had been gone over with a fine tooth comb and revealed nothing. Absolutely nothing. Whoever had wiped down the inside hadn't left a fingerprint, a strand of hair, anything. That took patience, attention to detail, and more knowledge of forensics than most people had. Given that nobody had witnessed anything when the car was stolen, and its tinted front window made it impossible for traffic cameras to get a good glimpse inside, the car was a complete dead end.

The report on the bridal shop was even worse. It had been a bomb, apparently a highly sophisticated one, that had taken out the store. Even trying to read the write up on it made his head hurt and his eyes cross.

Something was fishy about this whole thing. Whoever this guy was, he wasn't just some ordinary guy. Nor was he a low level thug. What he was pulling off took specialized skills, training. It was only through shear dumb luck, or possibly the grace of God, that Geanie was still alive.

What kind of beef could someone capable of these things have with Joseph, though? It made no sense. It was possible that whoever was after Geanie had just been hired by whoever wanted her dead. A hired assassin. That was the last thing any of them needed in their lives.

Liam came in looking so cheerful that Mark had a desire to punch him. He restrained himself, though, and instead handed him the reports. Liam skimmed them then looked up.

"See if you can get information out of someone, anyone, about killers that have used that kind of bomb," he said.

Liam raised an eyebrow. "You think someone hired this guy?"

"I'm thinking that's the best theory at the moment. I'm going to work on figuring out who might have hired him and I want you to work on figuring out who he might be. If we can catch either person, we can put an end to all this."

He had a sudden, horrific flashback to the whole Green Pastures mess. There it hadn't been enough to capture the man behind the assassins. In the end Mark had risked everything he was, everything he had, to beat the truth out of that man only to find there was no way to contact the killers to call everything off. A shiver went up his spine and he felt sick inside. Why was it that in his life, in his entire career, there was one horrific moment, one terrible choice, that kept coming back to torment him again and again?

And once again he was reminded that Paul had instigated it all, right before he went off and got killed by one of those very assassins.

"You okay?" Liam asked.

"No, I'm not," Mark said. What was it they said about the truth setting you free? If that was the case, why didn't he feel any better for admitting that?

He stood up abruptly. "Let's get moving. The wedding's a week from tomorrow. That's all the time the killer has which means we have even less."

"Understood." Liam sat down at his desk and immediately picked up the phone.

Mark grabbed his jacket and headed for the door, trying to shake the bad feeling that seemed intent on lingering and the images that kept replaying themselves like some hellish movie over and over again in his mind.

"It's all going to work out," he muttered as he got into his car.

It had to work out, anything else was unacceptable, even if it wasn't unthinkable.

He was headed to Joseph's. He had told him noon, but some things just wouldn't wait.

~

"Thank you again," Joseph said as he and Jeremiah stood still while tailors took measurements.

"For what?" Jeremiah asked, glancing down as one man tugged on his left pant leg.

"Where do I begin?" Joseph said with a shake of his head. "Being there for me, watching out for all of us, agreeing to be my best man, you name it."

"That's what friends are for," Jeremiah said, forcing a smile. It had been a long time since he was fitted for a suit like this and the sensation brought back a lot of memories, some good, most bad. At least Joseph had excellent taste when it came to tuxedos. These weren't just any tuxes. They were Armani that had been brought in especially for the wedding.

The other two groomsmen were going to be in that afternoon for their fittings. Jeremiah knew Joseph had wanted to have this taken care of all as a group, but plans had changed since the bombing of the bridal shop. Improvise was the word of the day. He just hoped that it didn't end up becoming the word of the entire wedding.

"So, tell me about the bachelor party," Joseph said, trying and failing to sound disinterested.

Jeremiah shook his head. "Nice try, but I'm afraid those plans are top secret."

"It's not going to be anything... you know... inappropriate, is it?" Joseph asked, looking slightly worried.

"I'm a rabbi, how much trouble could I get you into?"

"A lot," Joseph said without missing a beat.

Touché, Jeremiah thought. "I promise, nothing you'd be embarrassed to tell Geanie about."

"Good," Joseph said, looking immeasurably relieved. "I'm trusting you on this."

"Is that why you made me best man and not one of your other friends."

"No," Joseph said, a little too quickly. "Okay, the thought had crossed my mind, but to be honest, you and Cindy really are my best friends at this point. And, well, Geanie called dibs on Cindy."

"Just as well. I'd look terrible in a dress," Jeremiah joked.

"Ah, but I would pay good money to see that and laugh."

It was good that Joseph was keeping it together. Given what was happening the man could easily go to pieces and that would help no one, least of all Geanie.

The tailor jabbed Jeremiah with a pin and he bit back a sharp retort. Instead he cleared his throat and changed the subject. "So, it occurs to me that I'm your best man, and yet there are still things I don't know about you."

"Like what?"

"Like what you actually do for a living?"

Joseph laughed. "You're not the first to have trouble figuring that out."

"So, is it a deep, dark secret then?"

"Quite the opposite, actually. I oversee my investments, although most of the heavy lifting in that regard is done by other people. Same holds true for the companies I own thanks to my family. Most of my time is spent working with different charities, actually."

"I see."

"You know what the best part about having money is?" Joseph asked.

"What?"

"Giving it away," he said with a smile and a wink. "Honestly, that brings me almost as much joy as showing my dogs."

"And you really can't think of anyone who might be carrying a grudge? An ex-girlfriend, a distant relative, a former employee?"

Joseph shook his head. "The only girls I dated before Geanie are happily married. And I've never heard anything negative from any relative or employee. Certainly nothing in the last few years that even sticks out."

"You're a lucky man in that regard. It's not easy to go through life without making enemies, especially when you have the kind of position that you do."

Joseph shrugged. "I've always lived by the Golden Rule. Do unto others as you'd have done unto you. It's served me well."

"Any women who have pursued you that you've turned down?" Jeremiah asked.

"You think some sort of crazed stalker is doing this?" Joseph asked, looking if anything more bewildered than before.

"It's a theory. After all, whoever's doing this is going after Geanie, not you."

"Well, there was one woman who worked at one of the charities who seemed interested a couple of years ago. I let her down as gently as possible and she ultimately quit. I never heard anything from her since, though. I figured she'd moved on."

"Maybe, maybe not. At least that's someplace to start. You'll have to give Mark her name and what information you can about her so he can have her checked out."

"It's hard to believe that all of this can have something to do with a two-year-old crush."

"Stranger things have happened."

"Ouch!" Joseph exclaimed as he got stuck with a pin again.

"Stop!" Jeremiah commanded, loud enough to make everyone in the room jump.

Between the two of them they'd now been pricked by pins three times. Something about that seemed off to him. Good tailors wouldn't prick someone unless they were really rushing, incredibly nervous, or doing it on purpose.

"Back away," he growled at the man kneeling at his feet.

The man stood up, his face flushing and scurried back a couple of steps.

"You, too," Jeremiah ordered the man who was pinning Joseph's pants.

The man hesitated, eyes flicking to his comrade then back to Jeremiah.

"What's going on here?" the owner of the store hurried over, clearly concerned about the commotion.

"How long have these two worked for you?" Jeremiah demanded.

"About a week. They came highly recommended. Why? Is there anything wrong?"

Jeremiah glanced over at Joseph who had grown very pale. Sweat was beading on his forehead. Jeremiah himself was starting to feel a bit lightheaded.

"Very wrong," Jeremiah rasped as Joseph suddenly fell to his knees beside him. "Call 911 now! And tell them we've been poisoned."

8

The owner stared at Jeremiah, his mouth hanging open in shock. The tailor who was farthest away turned, knocked the man over, and headed for the front of the store. Jeremiah could feel himself weakening and knew there was no way he could catch him. The man who had been working on Joseph's pants was another story, though. He was only two feet away and there was terror written all over his face.

Jeremiah lunged forward, feeling his knees beginning to give way beneath him. The guy jumped back as Jeremiah began to fall, but he reached out, caught him around the knees, and took him down with him.

The man kicked out, one shoe grazing Jeremiah's shoulder. He ignored it and dragged himself up toward the man's head. The man was flailing wildly now, screaming. He should have had the brains to run when his friend did.

Jeremiah's vision was fading. He was moments from losing consciousness even as he heard Joseph hit the ground behind him.

He couldn't risk this man escaping while the owner pulled himself together and got the police on scene. Jeremiah grabbed the man's head, lifted it and then slammed it down into the ground with all the strength he had left.

The man stopped struggling instantly and Jeremiah fell on top of him. He should check on the pins, see if he could figure out what they were coated in, but he knew he couldn't move that far.

The owner of the shop was scrambling to his feet. "Poison?" the man asked, voice shaking.

"Yes, hurry," Jeremiah managed to whisper before darkness claimed him.

~

Mark had just walked in the front door of Joseph's house when his phone rang. "Excuse me," he told Cindy and Geanie as he answered it. It was Liam.

"What's happening?" he asked.

"Joseph and Jeremiah are being transported to the hospital. They were poisoned by two men at the tuxedo shop where they were being fitted."

"Poisoned?" Mark asked sharply. "Are you sure?"

"Paramedics confirmed it."

"Are they going to be okay?" Mark asked, turning away from Geanie and Cindy who had both gone pale.

"Too soon to tell. You'd better get down there. Jeremiah managed to knock out one of the men who did it."

"Should I go there or the hospital?" Mark asked, suddenly feeling quite helpless.

There was a lengthy pause before Liam said, "I'll oversee the interrogation when he gets here. You go to the hospital."

"Good idea," Mark muttered. Liam was a smart guy. "I'll get there as fast as I can."

He hung up and turned to the women who were staring at him in anguish. "There's been another attack, this time on the guys," he said. "They're heading to the hospital."

"Then so are we," Cindy said.

"They're not going to let you in to see them, not for a while."

"We can't sit here and wait," Geanie protested.

"Okay, let's go," Mark said.

~

Cindy had been waiting for what seemed like endless hours for Jeremiah to wake up. The doctors had assured her that he would, but that it was going to take a while given what had been put into his system.

In the room next door she knew Geanie was sitting with Joseph. She was guessing the other woman had had just as little sleep as she had. She stretched her neck and yawned, glancing at the doorway and thinking of going to check on Geanie.

She looked back just as Jeremiah's eyes fluttered open. He stared up at her for a moment. "Yapheh," he muttered.

Cindy didn't know what he said, but she was pretty sure it was in Hebrew. A surge of relief went through her. She knew what the doctors had said but seeing Jeremiah actually awake and talking meant she could finally breathe again. She put on a brave smile, hoping it looked calm and confident.

"We have to stop meeting like this," Cindy answered.

"You mean the hospital isn't your favorite date spot?" he slurred.

Her heart skipped a beat and she forced herself to take a deep breath. He was clearly still out of it.

"No, I generally prefer dinner, a movie, something like that," she said, forcing herself to keep her tone light.

"Sounds nice. We'll have to do that when this is all over."

Again she struggled to remain calm, but before she knew what she was doing she said, "Promises, promises."

"I'm not made of stone," he said.

Before she could ask him what that meant Mark came into the room. "You're awake," he said, sounding relieved.

Jeremiah nodded slowly. "Apparently." He swallowed hard and turned his head slightly to the side. "Where's Joseph?"

"He's okay. Still unconscious, but the doctors say he's going to be just fine."

"He got a bigger dose than me."

"Yes, well, neither of you received enough poison to kill you, just mess you up, knock you out."

"Why?" Cindy asked. "If the point wasn't to kill, why go through all that trouble?"

"That's what I'm trying to figure out," Mark admitted. "I've been wondering if sickness was the endgame or if someone was planning on kidnapping you guys once you were out cold. I'm just impressed you figured out what was happening in time to thwart the plan," Mark said, addressing the last to Jeremiah.

"I'm grateful, too," Jeremiah said.

"Well, we can talk about it later when you're a little bit more coherent," Mark said.

"Did you catch the guys?" Jeremiah asked.

"One of them. We're trying to get him to talk. Like I said, we'll know more a little later."

Cindy followed Mark out into the hall.

"Any luck with that guy?" she asked.

"All we know is that someone paid him and his friend to use these special pins to stick Joseph and Jeremiah with. The money was good enough that they didn't ask questions. His friend made the contact. He told us his name and we're trying to find him. Hopefully when we do he can shed some light on who is behind all of this."

Cindy nodded.

"Cheer up, at least this is the first real break we've had," Mark said. "We might just wrap this thing up before the wedding after all."

"The wedding," something went off in the back of Cindy's mind, something she was forgetting. "Oh gosh," she said, pulling out her phone to check the time.

"What is it?" Mark asked.

"We're supposed to pick up Geanie's parents and cousin at the airport in an hour," Cindy said.

Mark held up a hand. "I'll send someone for them. For now I don't want Geanie anywhere that isn't this hospital or Joseph's house. I want to know where she is at all times, and you, too, for that matter."

"Why me?" Cindy asked, startled.

"They didn't just poison Joseph. They poisoned Jeremiah, too."

"Yes, but that's because they had to knock out both of them if they wanted to snatch Joseph, otherwise Jeremiah would have stopped them."

"I know that, but I don't want to take any chances. After all, someone might get frustrated and decide to hurt you to get at them."

Cindy took a deep breath. "Okay."

"When you and Geanie are ready to go back to the house have one of the officers take you. I don't want to take chances. For all we know someone could or even already has sabotaged your car."

Cindy hunched her shoulders. Mark sounded paranoid, but she knew he was right. That's what scared her. She gave him the information for Geanie's arriving family and he left a minute later.

Cindy walked over to Joseph's room. There was a police officer stationed outside his room as well. He nodded at her as she walked inside. Geanie was sitting, holding Joseph's hand, and staring at him anxiously.

"He's going to be okay," Cindy reassured her.

"I know, I just want him to wake up."

"Well, hopefully it won't be long now. Jeremiah just woke up a couple of minutes ago."

Geanie's face scrunched up in anxiety. "I know Joseph had a higher dose than Jeremiah did. Who knows how much longer before he comes to?"

Cindy couldn't stand to see her friend in such distress. She sat down next to her and rubbed her back gently. "You'll never believe the crazy thing Jeremiah said when he woke up." She was hoping to distract Geanie from her fear.

"What?" Geanie asked, not taking her eyes off Joseph's face.

"I told him we needed to stop meeting like this and he asked me if the hospital wasn't my favorite place for a date."

"What?" Geanie asked, her eyes swiveling toward Cindy and opening wide.

Cindy smirked. Geanie was always pushing Cindy to get a love life, at least, since she'd gotten one. "I told him dinner and a movie was more my style."

"And what did he say?" Geanie asked, excitement creeping into her voice.

"That it sounded nice and we'd have to do that when this was all over."

Geanie dropped Joseph's hand and seized Cindy's shoulders, shaking her lightly. "I think he just asked you out!" she practically shouted.

Cindy winced, wishing Geanie weren't so loud.

"I don't think I'd go that far," she said.

"Oh no you don't, you're not getting out of this that easily," Geanie said. "You're going to tell me *everything*."

"There's not much more to tell. I teased him and he said he wasn't made out of stone, whatever that means."

"That means the man's annoying self-control is eroding!" Geanie said, jumping to her feet. "You have to take advantage of this. You have to make him take you out right away. Go back in there and get a commitment for a date." She grabbed Cindy's arm and tried to drag her to the door.

Cindy firmly planted herself in the chair, though, as panic raced through her. "No! I can't."

"Why not? This is the perfect opportunity! I'm telling you he asked you out."

"He was half-unconscious, out of his mind," Cindy protested.

"That's why you've got to follow up quickly before he can claim forgetfulness."

"But, I don't want to go out on a date with him."

"Liar!" Geanie hissed, her face contorting in sudden, unexpected fury.

"What?" Cindy gasped, taken aback.

"You heard me. You totally want to go out with him. It's the reason you won't even look seriously at another guy. You've been pining after Jeremiah for nearly two years now and it's time to put an end to it."

"We're just friends."

"Don't give me that crap. I know you too well. You and Joseph are friends. You and Mark are friends. You and Jeremiah are two people too afraid to admit that you're in love with each other because then you'd have to do something about it, and you're both terrified of what that would mean."

"You're wrong."

"Not about this. Your face lights up every time he enters the room. You can't even say his name without smiling, even when the topic is serious. To be honest all of us are getting sick of waiting for the two of you to wise up and do something about it."

"Who is 'all of us'?" Cindy asked.

"Everyone. Joseph, Mark, Traci, everyone on staff at the church. Dave even started a betting pool about how long it would take the two of you to kiss. Winner gets taken out to lunch by the losers."

"That's terrible!" Cindy said, horrified that her coworkers were betting on her love life.

"No, what's terrible is that I'm the only person who can possibly win at this point. Everyone else's dates have come and gone. I knew how stupidly stubborn you are, though, and how afraid of change. Ironically I never thought I'd win the bet because I didn't count on him being just as stupid."

"I don't have to sit here and listen to this," Cindy said, realizing she was shaking and that she was getting really angry.

"No, you don't. You can march next door and tell that man how you feel about him. That's what you would do if you weren't such a coward."

"It's complicated!" Cindy screamed, leaping to her feet.

"Can you guys stop shouting?" Joseph slurred.

They both turned and stared at him. His eyes were open and he was staring at them groggily.

"Oh, honey!" Geanie sobbed and threw herself half on top of him, hugging him fiercely.

"Careful," he whispered, but she didn't seem to hear or care.

Cindy just stared at the two of them as they were hugging. Her anger started to fade and in its place she felt a stab of jealousy. She could have hugged Jeremiah when he woke up, but she hadn't. It wasn't her place. She wrapped her arms around herself, feeling suddenly very cold.

All the excuses for why she and Jeremiah could never be together flashed through her mind. Some of them were valid, but the majority of them were just roadblocks she herself had put up, probably because she was afraid, just as Geanie had pointed out.

She should give the couple their privacy, but she wasn't ready to go back in the other room and face Jeremiah just yet, not with all the emotions that were cascading through her. Heaven only knew what she would say to him.

At last Genie sat back down in her chair, wiping her eyes.

"I'm glad to see you awake," Cindy said to Joseph.

"Glad to be awake. Alive. What happened?"

They filled him in to the best of their knowledge.

"So, how long have I been here?" Joseph asked at last.

"Almost twenty-four hours," Cindy said. "It's Saturday, almost noon."

Geanie started. "Oh my gosh! I haven't looked at the clock in hours. We have to pick up my parents. They'll be landing in like half an hour."

"Relax, Mark is handling that for us," Cindy said. "And he wants us to have a police officer drop us back at Joseph's when we're ready to go."

"You both have been here all night?" Joseph asked gently.

Cindy and Geanie nodded in unison.

"Then I think the best plan is for you to both get back to the house, shower, and be there to greet the family when they arrive. Heaven only knows they'll have a lot of questions, and it would be better if you were there to answer them."

"But, I don't want to leave you," Geanie protested.

"It's just for a few hours. I'm sure they'll let us out of here soon," he reassured her. "You can always come back later tonight to visit if we're still stuck here."

"It is a good idea," Cindy said gently. "There's a lot to do and we should be there to get your parents settled in. Mark wouldn't even know what rooms to put them in."

Geanie nodded reluctantly. "Okay, but we'll be back for dinner."

"Great, then you can smuggle me in some real food. Just, do me a favor?"

"Anything," Geanie said.

"Please don't bring your family. I don't want the first time we meet for me to be stuck in a hospital bed. Not exactly the first impression I was hoping for."

"You've got it," Geanie promised.

"I'll hold her to it," Cindy said with a smile.

"I'm counting on it. Now, get out of here you two. I'll see you both later."

They left Joseph's room and took a quick look in on Jeremiah. Fortunately there was a nurse there taking vital signs so Geanie didn't say anything Cindy would later have to kill her for. They told him the plan and he agreed it was a good one and that he'd see them when they were back later that night.

They left his room and approached the officer outside.

"Mark wanted someone to give us a ride back to Joseph's," Cindy explained.

"Just give me five minutes," he said. He spoke into his radio and in less than five minutes another uniformed officer arrived. He escorted them outside to a patrol car where his partner was waiting.

"I've never been in the back of a police car," Geanie admitted as she and Cindy climbed into the back.

The first officer chuckled. "Be grateful you're not in handcuffs. That's a whole different experience."

"Can you use the siren?" Geanie asked.

"Geanie," Cindy reproved gently.

"Sure, but we'll wait until we're almost there to do it."

"Sometimes I forget that deep down inside you're twelve," Cindy said with a shake of her head.

"Please, I'm not either twelve. I'm seven," Geanie said with a tired smile. "Look, I'm sorry I was so harsh on you back there."

"Let's just forget it. We're both tired and more than a little stressed," Cindy said, not wanting to rehash the gist of that fight in front of the officers.

"Okay. Deal," Geanie said, leaning her head back against the seat.

When they hit the bottom of Joseph's hill, true to their word, the officers put on the siren. Even Cindy found herself grinning from ear to ear as they raced up the hill as though in pursuit of some suspect.

At the top the patrolmen who were stationed outside the house were laughing and shaking their heads when the car pulled to a halt and Cindy and Geanie got out.

"Couldn't resist, could you?" one of them called.

"Why would you even want to try?" Geanie joked.

They made it into the house and Cindy realized as she climbed the stairs just how exhausted she was. She had slept fitfully at the hospital but that clearly had not been enough. As she dragged herself into her room she looked longingly at the bed. The truth was, though, they probably had just over an hour before family descended on them and they should be ready.

"I just want to sleep," she heard Geanie groan from the doorway next door.

"I hear you," Cindy muttered.

Still, forty-five minutes later she felt better as she headed back downstairs after having showered and changed into clean clothes. She had just reached the foyer when the front door flew open and a tall man with intense green eyes burst inside.

9

Cindy let out a little scream which appeared to startle the man even more than he had startled her. Behind her she heard running footsteps on the stairs.

"Dad!" Geanie shouted as she ran past Cindy and flung her arms around the man standing just inside the door. He hugged her back, lifting her off the ground.

When he put her down they both stepped further inside and allowed two others to come through the door. Geanie hugged first her mom then her cousin.

"How was your trip?" Geanie asked.

"Good. Plane actually landed early. I must say we were a bit surprised to get a police escort," her father said with raised eyebrows.

"Let's get you settled and then I'll tell you all about it," Geanie said. She turned to Cindy, "This is my Maid of Honor, Cindy. Cindy, my family."

"Pleased to meet you," Geanie's father said while the other two bobbed their heads up and down.

Cindy smiled and helped pick up some of the luggage that was piled on the porch.

"Okay, your rooms are on the second floor," Geanie said, leading the way up the stairs.

"It really is a big place," her mom commented, voice neutral. Cindy couldn't tell if the woman was impressed or not. It was hard to imagine she wouldn't be. The house was magnificent.

"Isn't Joseph here to greet us?" her father asked.

"He's...indisposed at the moment, but he can't wait to meet you," Geanie said a bit haltingly.

Cindy bit her lip. Geanie clearly had not shared any of the most recent events with her family. She was also somewhat surprised that Joseph hadn't met her parents before this. That seemed a bit odd to her. It wasn't like they couldn't have afforded to fly them out or go back to meet them. She'd have to ask Geanie about it later.

They reached the landing and instead of turning right like Cindy was used to, they turned left. They were soon in another dark wood paneled corridor that seemed a mirror image of the one on the other side.

The first door they came to Geanie opened and gave everyone a peek inside. "This is a guest office you guys can use if you need to do anything with computers, faxes, anything like that."

"Who has a guest office?" her mom muttered.

"A week from today I do," Geanie said brightly.

She closed the door and continued on.

"I thought we were going to be staying at your house," her cousin piped up.

"Yes, there was a last minute change of plans. That's part of that whole long story I have to tell you," Geanie said.

"It's much nicer here anyway," Cindy said, trying to be helpful. "There's a lot more room and everyone can have their own space, even their own bathroom."

Geanie opened the second door. "Mom, Dad, this is the room you'll be staying in."

They all piled into the room and began setting down luggage. The room was decorated with beautiful Victorian antiques. It was light and airy with huge windows that looked out at the trees. Cindy secretly suspected that Joseph must have given the best guest room to his soon to be in-laws. It would have seemed like a smart move, but Geanie's mother didn't seem to be all that approving.

"Okay, and just across the hall we have Charlotte's room," Geanie said.

She exited into the hall and walked across, leading everyone into Charlotte's room which definitely felt like something straight out of a castle. There was even a little balcony off the far wall.

"Doesn't this room just make you feel like a princess?" Geanie gushed.

"Yes," Charlotte said with a restrained smile.

"Tell you what? I'll give everyone a few minutes to get settled and freshen up then we can all meet back up downstairs."

"Sounds fine," her dad said.

Geanie nodded and then she and Cindy beat a hasty retreat back downstairs. They made it into the kitchen and Geanie hopped up on one of the stools at the breakfast bar and slumped with a long sigh.

"Are you okay?" Cindy asked.

"That didn't exactly go as I had planned. Originally I was going to pick them up at the airport, take them to our house, then we'd go out to dinner with Joseph."

"So they could finally meet him."

"That was the general idea."

"Well, they'll meet him tomorrow, it's not the end of the world," Cindy said.

Geanie just shook her head.

Cindy glanced toward the foyer just to make sure no one had followed them down. "Is everything...you know, okay with you and your folks?"

"My mother doesn't approve of my marrying a rich guy."

Cindy was sure for a moment she couldn't have heard right. She struggled not to crack a smile as she said, "I thought it was all mother's dreams that their daughters marry rich guys."

"Well, not my mother."

"Wow, that's ironic."

"Tell me about it."

"So, seeing Joseph's house before even meeting him is-"

"A disaster."

"Your dad seemed a little more okay with everything."

"I think he is, although I know he's reserving judgment until he meets Joseph."

"Well, that's a good thing because Joseph is sure to win him over. Everyone likes him."

"Except for someone out there who really, really doesn't," Geanie reminded her grimly.

"Well, you know, there's no accounting for taste," Cindy said, hoping to get Geanie to cheer up before her parents made a reappearance.

The other woman rolled her eyes, which was a start.

~

Mark scowled as he dropped the latest report onto the growing stack on his desk. He stood up, getting ready to leave when a hand touched his elbow.

He turned and was shocked to see Gretchen Dryer standing there, a large envelope in her hand. She had on no make-up and there were dark circles under her eyes like she hadn't slept. Her hair was pulled back into a ponytail. The few other times he'd seen her, she'd been the picture of sophistication. Now she looked more like a scared young girl.

"Miss Dryer, what can I do for you?" he asked, shocked to see her there.

"Can I sit?" she asked.

"Of course," he said, offering her the chair next to the desk as he sat back down in his.

She licked her lips, clearly nervous. Her fingers were practically kneading the envelope she was holding, clenching and unclenching around it.

"Have you...figured out who the boy was, the one who claimed to be my brother?"

He took a deep breath. "No, I haven't, but I'm still looking into it."

She nodded, but didn't seem to be terribly surprised. "My parents keep everything, you know."

"No, I was not aware," he said, wondering where she was going with all of this.

"There are boxes and boxes of things in the attic. Every drawing I ever made, all our old report cards, everything."

She took a deep breath and glanced down at the envelope. "I know this is going to sound crazy, but a couple of weeks ago I had a dream. I dreamed about my brother. Not my real brother, but the one who came back to us. I dreamed we were swinging on the playset outside that my grandfather had built for us when we were little. We were just swinging, talking, and then he stopped, and he turned and looked at me, and asked for my help."

She stopped and for a moment he didn't think she was going to continue. He didn't know what to say, so he just sat quietly.

"My help," she repeated. "He said I had to find out who he really was, that it was important."

"In the dream I asked him why it was important, but he wouldn't say, he just kept saying 'help me' over and over again until I woke up crying."

Tears began streaking down her cheeks and he quickly handed her a tissue. She wiped her eyes and seemed to pull herself back together.

"The next morning I went into the attic and I started going through all the old boxes. I told my mom I was thinking of getting into scrapbooking, so she wouldn't ask me what I was doing. She can't stand hearing anything about Paul maybe not being who he said he was."

"I remember," Mark murmured.

She pulled some papers out of the envelope. "After days of searching, I found a few things that I think are important."

She handed two papers to Mark. Both were school essays written out in longhand. "What are these?" he asked.

"The top one was from a month before Paul was kidnapped. The bottom one was from a month after that other boy came to us."

"The handwriting is completely different," Mark noted, astonished.

She nodded. "Except for the name at the top. That's the same on both. But you'll notice that on the second one, the rest of it is nothing like the name."

"Which implies he learned how to write your brother's name, but he didn't learn how to write like your brother."

"That's what I thought," she said.

Next she pulled out two school pictures, one of a younger boy, another of a boy a couple years older.

"The resemblance is strong," he admitted. "Strong enough to fool a grieving parent."

She nodded. "Look at his teeth, though."

Mark looked close until he saw what she was referencing. "The second picture has pointed incisors, the first does not."

She nodded. "My parents had those teeth filed down by the dentist before Paul, or rather, fake Paul, got braces."

Mark sucked in his breath sharply. With the picture of the fake Paul at a young age, maybe he'd have more luck scanning online databases. If he had access to some facial recognition software...

He took a deep breath. He was getting way ahead of himself.

"There's one more thing," she said, reaching into the envelope and pulling out a small Bible.

"This was a gift to my brother when he learned to read."

"You told me that the imposter refused to go to church."

"Yes, but take a look at what he did. I never saw this when I was a kid. I'm shocked that my parents didn't say anything to him about it."

Mark wasn't sure what he was supposed to be looking for but he flipped through the Bible until he came to a section where pages had been clearly torn out.

"What are these pages, do you know?" he asked.

She nodded. "Absolutely. He tore out the entire book of Matthew."

Mark stared at her, astonished. "Are you serious?"

She nodded. "The entire book is gone, and he wasn't any too subtle about it."

Mark continued to flip through. "There's writing on some of these pages, in the margins."

"Most of that would be my real brother, but I don't know if all of it is. The handwriting should be different, though."

"Do you mind if I hold onto these things for a while?"

"You can keep them," she said. "My parents will never go looking for them. I'm just hoping I've done enough to help you find out the truth."

"Thank you, I really appreciate this," he said, standing up and shaking her hand.

She nodded and turned to go.

Mark sat back down in his chair after she had left and buried his head in his hands. He'd been honest with Cindy and Jeremiah. He'd had every intention of letting this go. It didn't seem like the universe wanted him to, though.

After a minute he put everything back in the envelope and opened his right hand drawer. There, sitting on top, was the note urging him to ask him his real name.

"I will, okay," he whispered, to no one in particular. He put the envelope on top and slid the drawer closed.

He turned his eyes to the stack of reports on his desk. "Right now, though, I have something much more urgent to deal with."

He got up and headed to his car. His bad mood was now officially worse as he forced his mind back to the task at hand.

The stack of reports sitting back on his desk all added up to one thing. It was definitely a professional assassin out to destroy Joseph's wedding. They weren't talking about some low-level thug or hitman either. Whoever this was had a lot of experience and a lot of money backing them up. All of which begged the question who could afford to hire him? And, perhaps even more pressing, how come he kept failing?

Maybe the point wasn't to kill either Geanie or Joseph but to make their lives a living hell. Still, why hire someone of this man's obvious skills for what ultimately ended up being a monumental case of harassment? Yes, two people had died, the women in the bridal shop, but they were in the wrong place at the wrong time, and the more Mark uncovered the more he became convinced that the assassin hadn't been trying to kill Geanie. He just wanted to terrorize her and he didn't care who got killed in the process.

All of which was terrible news for everyone around Joseph and Geanie at that moment. He began to seriously rethink his decision to have the bridal party staying in the mansion with them. After all, killing the mother-of-the-bride would certainly bring the festivities to a screeching halt.

Maybe he could convince them to postpone the wedding. If they did that, though, the killer might just slip away only to resurface a few months later when the wedding was back on.

Any way he looked at it he was starting to get a very bad feeling that this wedding was going to have the ultimate party crasher.

He walked into the hospital and headed straight for Jeremiah's room. He wanted to talk a few things over and the rabbi seemed a better choice than Joseph. He wondered fleetingly how things were going back at the mansion with Geanie's family. He could only imagine the fear they were experiencing as they walked into this nightmare. The others were at least getting used to this kind of insanity, sad as that was.

His phone rang and he was pleased to see that it was Traci. "Hey, honey, how are you doing?" he asked.

"Okay, although it turns out morning sickness? Not such an accurate description."

Mark furrowed his brow. "I'm sorry. I wish there was something I can do."

"Next time you can hold my hair for me," she said.

"In a heartbeat. That's what love is all about."

"I miss you," she said.

"I miss you, too."

"How about when you finish with all of this we go away on a real vacation, just the two of us."

"That sounds like a wonderful plan," he said.

"Ugh. Gotta go," she said before unceremoniously hanging up.

Mark felt bad for her as he pocketed his phone.

He checked in with the officers outside Jeremiah and Joseph's rooms, and they reported that all had been quiet since Cindy and Geanie had left. He pushed open the door to Jeremiah's room, took two steps inside, and froze.

The rabbi was gone.

~

Jeremiah was slouching in a chair next to Joseph's bed, chatting with him when Mark came flying in, eyes wild.

"Hi," Jeremiah said as Mark came to a stop.

"What are you doing in here?" the detective demanded.

"Talking to Joseph."

"How did you get in here?"

"I crawled out my window, shimmied along the ledge, and came in this one," Jeremiah said.

"What?"

He rolled his eyes. "I walked, from my room the five steps to this one. Why?"

"No one saw you do that," Mark said, turning red.

"I don't know why," Jeremiah said.

Actually, he knew exactly why. He had made sure the policemen outside didn't see him. The last thing he needed was to feel confined to his room. Besides, he'd wanted some time to talk to Joseph in private.

Mark went back into the hallway and Jeremiah could hear him reading the baffled officers the riot act. He didn't actually feel bad. If he could sneak out of his room and into Joseph's without their knowing, whoever was after Joseph could certainly get to him as well.

A minute later Mark returned. He looked like he was barely managing to restrain himself. He took a deep breath and sat down in the other chair in the room. "Next time you feel like taking a little walk, please inform the officers and for heaven's sake let one of them escort you."

"I'm not the one he's after," Jeremiah said calmly.

"No, but neither does he mind collateral damage," Mark snapped.

"Fair enough."

Joseph cleared his throat. "Yesterday, before all this happened, Jeremiah and I were discussing possible suspects. The only one that came to mind was a woman who worked for one of my charities two years ago who had a crush on me. I let her down easy, but she was still upset."

"Did she have money?" Mark asked.

Joseph blinked. "I have no idea, why?"

"Because I think you have a professional after you and they don't come cheap."

"I thought it was important Joseph bring her up," Jeremiah said.

"Okay, what's her name?" Mark asked.

"Amanda. Last name started with a B I believe. If you help me find my wallet I can give you a card of the person who can get you the last contact info we had for her."

Jeremiah watched as Mark checked the closet. The tuxedo pants he'd been wearing when they brought him in were hanging there. "Nothing here," Mark said.

Joseph craned his neck to look. "My wallet was in my pants that I had to take off to put those on. Do you think it's still at the store?"

Mark shook his head. "Officers collected your belongings. I've got them at the precinct. I didn't think about it until this minute."

"I'd like my wallet back," Jeremiah said evenly. He'd already checked his room looking for it and he'd been hoping the police had it.

"Sure," Mark said absently.

"You'll find a business card for The Coulter Foundation in my wallet. Ask for Miles in Human Resources and he'll be able to help you out."

"Okay, I'll do that as soon as I get back," Mark said. "Have either of you come up with any other possibilities of someone who might want to ruin this wedding?"

Both Jeremiah and Joseph shook their heads.

There was a sudden commotion outside and then a man burst into the room chased by two police officers. "Please, you've got to help me!" he screamed.

Jeremiah sat up abruptly. It was the second tailor, the one who had poisoned him.

"Help me!"

"What's going on?" Mark roared.

"He knows, he knows I failed and he's afraid I'll-"

The man fell to the ground convulsing. Just as suddenly as he had started, he stopped. His eyes rolled back in his head.

Mark dropped to the ground checking for a pulse but Jeremiah already knew he wouldn't find one.

The tailor was dead.

10

Cindy heard voices on the stairs. "I think everyone's coming down," she told Geanie.

Geanie sighed. "Okay, time to put on our game faces and tell them what's going on."

"Would you like some privacy, because I can always-"

"Oh no you don't! You're in this with me," Geanie said.

"Somehow, I was afraid of that," Cindy answered with a sigh. "Game faces it is," she said, plastering on the best fake smile she could manage.

They hopped down off their stools in the kitchen and walked into the entry way as Geanie's family was walking down the stairs.

"Let's head into the sitting room so we can all get comfortable," Geanie said brightly as soon as they had made it all the way down.

She turned and led the way into the sitting room where she picked one of the chairs. Cindy sat down on one of the couches and the others made themselves comfortable as well.

"Would anyone like anything to drink, coffee, tea, soda?"

"What, he allows something other than champagne into his house?" her mom said snidely.

"We're fine for now," her father said.

Geanie nodded. "First things first. Sorry about the hasty introductions earlier. This is Cindy Preston, my best friend and roommate. Cindy, these are my parents, Milt and Dorothy. And, of course, my cousin, Charlotte, is the one bridesmaid you haven't met yet."

"Nice to finally meet everyone," Cindy said.

"We've heard a lot about you," Dorothy said.

"It's nice to meet you," Milt said. At least he smiled.

Charlotte just dipped her head in acknowledgment.

"Okay, so we've got some catching up to do," Geanie said, her voice suddenly very nervous. "Obviously plans have changed somewhat."

"Somewhat?" Dorothy asked with a raised eyebrow.

As much as Cindy wanted to like Geanie's parents, she had to admit she was starting to feel less than charitable toward Dorothy. For just a moment she wished that she and Geanie had come up with some cover story: their house was being fumigated or something, just to spare the other woman from having to tell her annoying mother the truth.

Unfortunately, the lie wouldn't have held up more than a few hours. The constant police escort couldn't be explained away.

"Yes, well, the truth is, there have been some rather unfortunate accidents that have occurred in the last couple of days."

"What type of accidents?" Milt asked sharply, glancing at Cindy.

"Well, the bridal shop where I was having my dress fitted sort of...blew up for one," Geanie said with a nervous laugh.

"Blew up? For real?" Charlotte asked.

Geanie nodded.

"Are you okay?" Milt asked.

"I'm fine. I was knocked unconscious, but the only damage done was to the dress," Geanie said.

Cindy winced, thinking of the dress. In all the chaos, what Geanie was going to do for a wedding dress at this point was something they still had to figure out. They didn't have much time left either.

"Oh dear," Dorothy said, actually looking distressed.

"Yeah, so between that and a couple of other things, Cindy's detective friend thought it best we all just stay here until the wedding is over. Joseph's got a great security system after all."

"I don't understand," Milt said, leaning forward. "What does that have to do with anything?"

Geanie cleared her throat and looked at Cindy who nodded encouragingly.

"Well, the thing is. It looks like the shop wasn't an accident. The police think someone might be, I don't know, trying to sabotage the wedding or something."

It was downright painful to watch Geanie, who was always so blunt and forthcoming, dance around the truth with her parents.

"What?" Charlotte gasped.

"I knew this wedding was a terrible idea!" Dorothy burst out.

Milt jumped to his feet. "Where is Joseph? I think I'd like to have a word with him right now."

"That's just it, you can't." Geanie took a deep breath. "Yesterday while they were having their tuxes fit, he and the best man were poisoned. They're both in the hospital."

Milt sank slowly down into his chair, a look of shock on his face.

"Someone's trying to kill you?" Dorothy asked after a moment.

"We don't know that for sure," Cindy spoke up. "What we do know is that they are targeting Geanie and Joseph and trying to derail the wedding for some reason."

"I knew you'd come to no good carrying on with a rich California playboy," Dorothy said, wagging her finger at her daughter.

"I'm not 'carrying on' with him and he's not a playboy," Geanie said heatedly.

Suddenly everyone seemed to be shouting at once. For her part Cindy wished the ground would just open and swallow her whole as she listened to the escalating anger and accusations. After a minute everyone was on their feet and the shouting was just getting louder.

Sooner or later the patrolmen outside are going to come in here to see what all the commotion is about, Cindy thought. Images of them bursting in, guns drawn, danced through her head. This was so not good. Geanie didn't need this. Not one week before the biggest day of her life. Not when someone was trying to hurt or kill her. Not when family and friends should be loving and supporting her. It wasn't right.

And as Maid of Honor, she had a responsibility to stop it.

"Enough!" Cindy roared, leaping to her feet. "Everyone sit down and shut up!"

Everyone turned and stared at her as if she had grown a second head. "Right now!" she emphasized. "Sit!"

Slowly everyone else sat back down, eyes still riveted on her.

"You've all talked or shouted. Now you're all going to listen. First. Geanie and Joseph are in love and it couldn't have happened to two nicer people. Second. One week from today they are getting married regardless of what else happens or who is or isn't present for it. Third. When someone is a victim, you don't attack them. You love them, support them, and help them get through the experience while you do everything in your power and pray as fervently as you can that the bad guy gets caught. Fourth. Geanie is a grown woman and she can do whatever she wants. She is loving, sweet, funny, incredibly spiritual, and makes excellent choices. If you have a shred of decency in your hearts or a bit of love for her, you'll cut the crap and shower her with nothing but love and support until this is all over. Fifth. Anyone who can't live with what I just said doesn't need to be here and I will personally call one of the police officers from outside and have them put your butt on a plane out of here. Are we clear?"

Everyone else nodded mutely.

"Good. Now, I'm starving. Let's all get some lunch and talk about something happy for the next hour."

"You're the boss," Milt said.

"That's right, I am. Now, everyone follow me to the kitchen."

Cindy turned and stalked out of the room, head held high. After a few steps Geanie caught up to her. She grabbed her arm and squeezed it. "You were amazing in there," she breathed.

"Maid of Honor. It's my job to get you through the wedding and I take it seriously," Cindy said.

~

"Do we have no security here?" Mark demanded as he stood up. The man on the floor was dead. The way his own heart was racing he was afraid for a moment he was going to have a heart attack and join him.

"That's the other tailor, the one who got away. He must have been desperate to come here. Someone didn't want you questioning him," Jeremiah said from his chair.

"No, really?" Mark demanded, his voice dripping sarcasm.

Mark turned and barked at the two police officers. "One of you get me a doctor, and I mean like yesterday."

One of the officers scurried off and Mark threw himself down in the chair. "This is a fine mess," he said.

Less than a minute later the officer returned dragging a protesting doctor behind him. The man's protests stopped completely when he saw the corpse on the floor. He started forward.

"Don't waste your time, he's dead," Mark said bluntly. "I'm guessing that when you do an autopsy you'll discover that it was the same poison that he used on these two that did it."

"Obviously in a much higher dosage," Jeremiah said.

The rabbi was too calm. It rattled Mark at the moment.

"I've got to-"

"I'll tell you what you've got to do," Mark interrupted the doctor. "You've got to give me whatever staff or equipment I need to move these two men to a more secure location."

"I, I can't-"

"You can and you will. Tell me what I need."

The doctor picked up Joseph's chart and flipped through it with shaking hands. Finally he looked up. "The danger should be over. Let me see what I'd have to do to be able to release them."

"Do it and make it quick. Every second they're here they're at risk and so is everyone in this hospital," Mark said, glaring for good measure.

The doctor stumbled out of the room.

"Good call," Jeremiah said quietly.

"Not a word from you at the moment, okay?"

Jeremiah nodded.

Mark stood and began to pace. Things were spinning out of control. Or maybe it was just that *he* was spinning out of control. Either way he needed to lock this situation down and the only way he could do that was to get Joseph and Jeremiah back to the mansion and triple the police detail he had on them. If the captain put up a fight he'd just remind him that Joseph was so rich that his taxes alone probably paid for a quarter of their annual operating budget.

"It's going to be okay," Mark said to the air.

He would give anything to believe that was true.

~

Half an hour later Cindy had Geanie's parents recounting embarrassing stories about Geanie as a kid. Some of them were priceless. She was just sorry Joseph was missing out on hearing some of them. Although, she supposed there'd be plenty of time for that later. Plus, she'd make sure to tell him one or two of her favorites just to be on the safe side. Geanie was flushed scarlet but she was laughing as hard as the rest of them.

"I can't believe Joseph doesn't have a cook," Dorothy said as she bustled around the kitchen.

"I hope he doesn't expect you to cook," Milt said wrinkling his nose in a way that let Cindy know he, too, had had the misfortune of tasting Geanie's cooking.

"No, he cooks, and he's good at it. Can you believe that?" Geanie gushed.

"He cooks?" her mom asked incredulously. "You hang onto that one."

"I know, right?"

They had foregone the leftover cold cuts in the refrigerator and instead they were grilling some steaks they had found in the freezer on the cooktop range. Off to the side in a pan Dorothy was frying up some potatoes and onions. The smells were making Cindy start to salivate and she began to realize that the last thing she'd had to eat was some lousy hospital cafeteria food the night before. She couldn't even remember eating that much of it so she was definitely past due.

"Medium rare okay for everyone?" Milt asked, wielding some gourmet salt and some ground garlic like a pro.

"Yes, please," Geanie said.

"So, what happened?" Cindy asked, prompting Dorothy to finish her story.

"Well, we found her, sitting in the living room. She had painted her entire arm from shoulder to fingernails blue and she was getting ready to start painting one of her legs red. That's when we knew we had an artist on our hands."

"Yup, and that was just last Easter," Milt said with a straight face.

"Dad!" Geanie protested while Cindy and Charlotte giggled.

"Please tell me the food's almost ready," Cindy finally begged.

"Steaks are," Milt said, sounding supremely satisfied as he piled them high on a serving platter he'd found in one of the cupboards.

"So are the potatoes," Dorothy said as she reached for a bowl.

They took the food to a kitchen table where Cindy had already laid out plates and utensils for everyone.

"Ribeyes, I could get used to this," Milt said after taking his first bite.

"So, tell us more about the wedding. You've been awfully secretive," Dorothy said to Geanie.

Geanie grinned. "I've been trying to keep a lot of it as a surprise."

"Even Joseph doesn't know half of what's going on," Cindy corroborated.

"A mystery wedding. Sounds exciting," Dorothy said.

"Just as long as the time and place aren't a mystery," Milt joked.

"Well, I've got my dress, so we know forest green plays a part," Charlotte said.

"That is one of my colors, yes," Geanie admitted.

Cindy smirked. She knew the other one was fuchsia because that's what color her dress was.

"Practically the whole community is going to be there," Cindy said. "I've never heard of a wedding this huge."

"We didn't want to exclude anyone from the church," Geanie explained.

"And they all said yes."

"Should be something else," Milt said.

They fell silent as they all dug into their food. Cindy cleaned her plate before sitting back and taking a deep breath. She really had been starving as it turned out. Geanie reached for a second steak so clearly she had eaten less the night before than Cindy even.

"I can't wait for you to meet Joseph," she said.

"Well, can't we go over to the hospital a little later?" Milt asked.

Geanie wrinkled up her nose. "He really wanted to make a better first impression than that. I know he's nervous about meeting you guys and he wants everything to be perfect."

"Is he always so particular?" her mom asked, but her voice wasn't harsh, mostly curious.

"Not about most things. He's usually very easy going. Every once in a while, though, he wants things to be special and he spends a lot of time planning them. We were supposed to go to dinner tonight at the restaurant where he proposed to me. I know he's disappointed that's not happening," Geanie said.

"We'll be here for a few days, we can go another night," Milt said.

"I hope so, but there's a lot that's getting packed in starting tomorrow."

"Starting tomorrow?" Cindy joked. "There's a lot that's been packed in already."

"Well, yes, that's true," Geanie said with a tight smile.

Cindy reached over and grabbed her hand. "Don't worry, it will all get done."

"Yes, and we're here to help," Dorothy said, grabbing Geanie's other hand."

"Thanks, guys."

"Well, this is all very touching," Milt said with a twinkle in his eye. "I think, though, we'll have to be let in on a few of the big wedding secrets to really be helpful."

"Oh, you think you're getting information out of me that easily?" Geanie said.

"It's worth a try," he said with a smile and a shrug.

Cindy was so grateful that all of the crazy tension from earlier seemed to have calmed down. She just prayed it didn't return.

Suddenly in the distance Cindy could swear she heard a siren. She swiveled her head around. "Does anyone else hear that?" she asked after a moment.

The others nodded.

"It sounds like it's turning up the hill," Geanie said, somewhat breathlessly.

The siren cut out suddenly.

Cindy turned and headed for the front door, the others trailing behind her. She stepped outside and heard the sound of engines.

"Is someone coming?" she asked the officer who was nearby.

"Yes, Mark called a minute ago to let us know he was heading up the hill."

"Who is Mark?" she heard Dorothy ask.

"Cindy's friend the detective. He and his wife are coming to the wedding," Geanie said quietly.

A hush fell as the roar of the engines grew louder. A sense of anticipation was building, but why Cindy could not say. Her stomach was also beginning to knot up. Why had Mark not called her? Had something gone wrong and he wanted to tell them in person? Is that why they'd heard the siren?

A minute later Mark's car came into view. He pulled up in front of the house and got out just as an ambulance turned the corner. It was moving more slowly and it parked behind him finally.

"What's going on?" Milt asked.

Cindy shook her head. She didn't know, but she was worried.

Two paramedics hopped out of the front of the truck and ran around to open up the back. They disappeared inside and a moment later they reappeared carrying a stretcher with someone on it. Two more paramedics who must have been riding in the back carried another stretcher out right behind it.

They walked up and set the stretchers down right in front of them.

Cindy looked down at the first one and saw a familiar face.

"Okay," Joseph said with a wince. "This is more than a little embarrassing."

11

"Joseph!" Geanie shrieked and threw herself half on top of him.

"Easy," he grunted.

Cindy looked past him to see Jeremiah laying on the second stretcher, a look of incredible irritation on his face.

Before she could go to him, though, Mark interrupted. "Let's get these two inside. It was hard enough to force the doctor to release them early, we don't need to injure them further before we even make it into the house."

Everyone hastened back inside and the paramedics carried Joseph and Jeremiah in on the stretchers.

"Their orders are to rest and recline as much as possible for the next forty-eight hours until everything has worked out of their systems," Mark said.

"This is certainly a surprise," Cindy said.

"Yeah, well, there's a reason for that," Mark said darkly.

"So should we take them to their bedrooms?" the lead paramedic asked.

"No!" Joseph practically shouted. He cleared his throat. "Please. There are some couches in the living room. That would be better, I think. Closer to the kitchen, you know and...everything."

"I agree," Jeremiah said.

Geanie led the way and within minutes the paramedics had transferred each man to one of the couches. As soon as they were out of the room, Jeremiah sat up. "I need a shower," he grumbled.

"I promised the doctor nothing so strenuous until tomorrow," Mark said.

Jeremiah glared at him and Mark rolled his eyes. "Fine. You had less poison than Joseph." He turned to Joseph. "But no shower for you until tomorrow."

Joseph nodded, looking suddenly very tired. "I'd like to sit up for a while, though, and get something to eat."

"That much I can allow," Mark said with a sigh. "When did I become the keeper for the two of you?"

"When you forcefully checked us out of the hospital," Jeremiah said.

"Bullying that doctor in the process," Joseph said as he struggled to sit up. He finally made it, but his face looked wan.

"What on earth happened?" Cindy asked.

"We'll get to that in a minute," Joseph said. He pushed himself up to a standing position, swaying slightly on his feet as he did so. For a moment Cindy thought he was going to fall down, but he managed to stay upright. After he stabilized he stretched out his hand. "Hello, I'm Joseph Coulter," he said.

"Milt," Geanie's father said, stepping forward to shake his hand.

"Dorothy," her mother said, following suit.

"You can call me cousin Charlotte," the other woman said, shaking his hand last.

"It's wonderful to meet you all," Joseph said, clearly trying to summon as much dignity as possible given the circumstances. "I had hoped-"

"Forget about it," Milt said with a wave of his hand. "You know what they say about the best laid plans of mice and men."

Joseph smiled. "I do indeed."

"You sit right back down there and we'll bring you some lunch. Both of you," Dorothy said, encompassing Jeremiah with her glance.

"I think I can agree to that," Jeremiah said. "Hi, I'm the best man."

"He sure is," Joseph said fervently. "He saved my life."

Milt and Dorothy hurried into the kitchen to get some food.

"So, what did bring you guys here?" Cindy directed her question at Mark.

"We found the other tailor. Or, actually, he found us. Came running into the hospital screaming for help before he dropped dead. Obviously tests have to be run, but we suspect that a much larger dose of what Jeremiah and Joseph received was to blame."

"Oh my," Geanie said, sinking down on the couch to sit beside Joseph. She took his hand in hers. "I'm glad you're alright."

"That's when I decided I wanted everyone where I could keep an eye on them," Mark said. "Obviously postponing the wedding wouldn't really solve anything, so I want to lock everything down as much as possible."

"Well, it looks like you've got a good handle on that," Cindy said.

"Not yet. I'm going to send officers to collect the rest of the bridal party. We're not going to be taking any chances."

"There's plenty of room," Joseph said.

Geanie pursed her lips. "I'm not sure how Melissa and Veronica are going to feel about that."

"Frankly, I don't care how they feel. That's what's going to happen," Mark said. "I'll need their addresses so I can send officers for them. Same with the groomsmen. What are their names?"

"Jordan and Dave."

"Dave? Not Wildman, the youth pastor?"

"That's the one."

Mark rolled his eyes. "At least I don't know Jordan."

"Oh, you'll love him," Cindy said, trying to suppress a grin.

"Great," Mark said sarcastically. "That means he's another crazy First Shepherd person."

"We prefer the word eccentric," Geanie said with a smirk.

Milt and Dorothy returned. "Are steaks and fried potatoes okay?" Dorothy asked.

"Sounds wonderful," Jeremiah said.

"We cut the steaks up into bite sized pieces so you wouldn't have to try to juggle the plate and the knife," Milt said.

"Thank you, that was exceptionally thoughtful," Joseph said, smiling as he took his plate. "Are these the ribeyes from the freezer by any chance?"

"Yes, we helped ourselves. I hope you don't mind," Dorothy said.

"Not at all. I think it's great. I was planning a big barbeque for tomorrow, but I don't think my 'keeper' is going to let me stand for that long. We'll just do something else tomorrow."

"We can always order pizza," Geanie said brightly.

"I need to go check on some things. I'll be back in a few hours. Anything I need to know before I head out?" Mark asked.

"Yes!" Cindy said, jumping to her feet. "I almost forgot to show you what Geanie found."

He followed her out into the entry and then around the stairs where she showed him the black rose with the card. "We figure the intruder left it right before I discovered him," she explained.

Mark nodded. He went out to his car and returned with an evidence bag which he carefully put the rose in. "I'll have this tested and see what we can find out."

"What is it?" Jeremiah asked, walking in slowly.

"You're supposed to be relaxing, or at least eating," Mark snapped.

"I wanted to know what you found."

Mark showed him the rose and Cindy could swear Jeremiah actually looked startled. He recovered momentarily, though, and asked, "What does the card say?"

"No happy endings," Cindy reported. "I believe the intruder left it."

"Of course he did," Jeremiah said, so softly she wasn't sure if she'd heard right.

"What is it?" Mark asked sharply.

Jeremiah shook his head. "A very bad feeling, that's all."

Cindy was sure it had been more than that but decided to press him for information later when they were alone.

"Okay, I'll be back in a little while. We've got a lot to talk about," Mark said.

"You've found something else out," Cindy said, grabbing his arm.

"I have, but not pertinent to this case."

"Paul?" she breathed.

He nodded. "We'll talk later. I need to get the boys at the lab analyzing this as soon as possible. Hopefully, they'll come up with something."

"But you don't think they will," she said, reading it in his face.

"No, I don't," he admitted. "I think whoever's doing all this is a professional, hired by someone, and he's not going to be careless. Now, I'll see you later," he said, a little more forcefully.

Cindy nodded and let go of his arm. She took a step back and felt Jeremiah touch her back. They had a lot to talk about, too. She wanted to hear more about the tailor who had just died. Hopefully if the killer hadn't left evidence on the rose, he'd left some on the body.

"Do you need the contact info for the bridal party?" she asked.

"Yeah, text it to me."

"Okay."

Mark nodded and went out the front door. She pulled her phone out of her pocket and texted him the information he'd need so he'd have it right away. Finished, she turned to Jeremiah. "Let's go back with the others. You should finish your food."

He nodded and together they turned and went back into the living room. Cindy was relieved to see that everyone seemed to have been getting along just fine in their absence.

Milt looked up when they entered the room. "Joseph was just telling us that they have you to thank for getting them together," he said to Cindy.

She smiled. "I knew they would be perfect for each other. I just provided an opportunity for them to see each other in a social setting and the rest they worked out for themselves."

"So, how did you propose?" Dorothy asked.

Cindy was surprised that Geanie hadn't told her parents that back when she got engaged. Given their reaction earlier, though, maybe it hadn't been easy.

"Well, we had been dating for five months, and every month we went somewhere nice to celebrate our anniversary, or 'monthaversary' as we called them. I had decided to propose the month before, but it took me a while to find the perfect ring and to figure out the perfect way to do it," Joseph said.

"You'd been thinking about it for a whole month?" Geanie asked, looking at him in amazement.

"I knew around St. Patrick's Day," Cindy said.

Geanie picked up a pillow and lobbed it at her. Cindy caught it and threw it back with a laugh.

"Anyway, I took her to Rue de Main, a French restaurant here in town that is just wonderful. What she didn't know, was that all the other diners were people I had hired to be there. I'd actually borrowed a choir from another church across town because I didn't want her recognizing anyone."

"It worked," Geanie said with a smile.

"After the waiter brought our appetizer, the whole restaurant jumped up and sang 'Masquerade' from Geanie's favorite play, The Phantom of the Opera. They sang, and danced and even had little masks they were using."

"It was unreal," Geanie said with a laugh. "I thought Joseph had organized some crazy flash mob. I was laughing and squealing all at the same time. When they were done, everyone went back to eating as though nothing had happened."

"I once heard Geanie complain that she wished life was more like a musical where people burst into song spontaneously."

"It was so cool. I thought that was it, though," Geanie admitted.

"Then, when the salad course came out, a couple got up and sang 'Music of the Night', also from Phantom," Joseph said.

"It was so romantic, I was just dying," Geanie said.

"Then, when they brought out the entrees, a different couple got up and sang 'All I Ask of You'," Joseph said.

"That's when I started to get the teeniest bit suspicious that this might all be leading somewhere," Geanie admitted. "I was stunned and entertained, and just swept away all at the same time."

"All part of the plan," Joseph said with a grin. "Then, the waiter brought dessert out. Another couple began to walk toward us singing 'The Point of No Return'. Geanie turned to look at them."

"When I turned back to Joseph he was on one knee holding this ring," Geanie said, lifting her hand.

Cindy had seen the ring many times. The diamond was actually heart-shaped and set in a heart-shaped setting. It was exquisite.

"I was so breathless, I couldn't even say 'yes'. I just kept nodding over and over again and smiling, and crying."

"I took that to mean 'yes', and apparently I was right," Joseph said, leaning over to kiss Geanie.

"That is beautiful," Dorothy said, tears shining in her own eyes.

"Afterwards, everyone shook our hands and congratulated us. It was unbelievable."

"And you hired that entire choir?" Milt asked, shaking his head.

Joseph smiled. "I'd heard they were trying to raise money for new choir robes. I contacted the director and offered to buy him new robes in exchange for the serenading. Plus, everyone got fed, so it seemed like a mutually beneficial arrangement."

"That's amazing," Charlotte breathed, still glassy-eyed.

"Yeah, those people are coming to the wedding, but we promised them that this time they could just be part of the audience and not the entertainment," Geanie said with a laugh.

"I think they were actually a little disappointed by that," Joseph joked.

Jeremiah actually smiled. "I don't think anyone could have topped that," he said.

"You definitely set the bar," Geanie said with a smile.

The phone rang and Geanie hopped up to answer it.

She returned a minute later. "That's the wedding planner. She wants to come over in an hour to discuss some more things."

"Am I going to be part of this discussion?" Joseph asked, "or is this more of your secret stuff?"

"No, you can be part of it."

"I really should get cleaned up."

"You heard Mark. Not until tomorrow," Jeremiah said. "I, on the other hand, am heading upstairs to do exactly that."

"I hate you right now," Joseph lamented.

~

Mark had a bad feeling about the rose that he dropped off with forensics. He warned them to check for poison on the thorns, just in case. Then he met up with Liam who looked grim.

"What do you have?" he asked.

"I called a friend who called a friend who called an uncle who was able to help out with some information."

"Okay."

Liam handed him four pictures. "He could find references to that particular poison being used by four different professionals. One Russian, two Middle Eastern, and one American."

"Unless whoever has a grudge against Joseph has connections overseas, let's assume that the American is our man."

"Our woman, actually," Liam said, bringing one of the pictures to the top. "Sonja, no last name."

The picture was unbelievably blurry, but showed a woman with short dark hair and sunglasses.

"This is it? This is what we have to work with?"

"I know, it's not much, but apparently she specializes in revenge killings, usually ex-husbands."

Mark sighed. "It's past time that we visited Joseph's crush girl. Maybe she sent this woman after him."

"I'm free now," Liam said.

"Great, let's do this."

As it turned out, Amanda lived almost half an hour outside Pine Springs, halfway between it and Los Angeles proper. Her house had a for sale sign on the front lawn with a large SOLD sticker placed across it.

Fortunately, she was home. She answered the door, a kerchief covering her blonde hair. Her fingers had two inch long fingernails, three of which looked to have broken off recently.

"House is already sold," she snapped.

"That's not why we're here," Mark said, pulling out his badge.

"Oh," she said, looking startled and falling back a step.

"May we come in?" Liam asked.

She glanced behind her, eyes seeming to dart around. "This really isn't a good time."

"That's okay, this will just take a few minutes," Mark said, forcing a friendly smile across his face.

"Um, okay, but it's got to be fast. I'm, uh, expecting company," she said, stepping back to let them in.

"Thank you. We'll be out of your hair before you know it," Mark said.

They stepped into the house which was piled everywhere with boxes.

"Congratulations on the house sale. It just happened?" Liam asked.

"No, it closed last week. My stupid realtor wanted to keep the sign up as long as possible, though. Apparently it's good for his business."

"You closed, but haven't had to move out yet?" Mark asked.

"Nah, it was in the contract. Buyers knew I needed an extra few weeks to pack up all my stuff. It's just me, I don't have anyone to help do that," she said, leading them into a living room. There was a door at the far end that she hastened over and closed.

Mark and Liam exchanged a glance.

"Bathroom's a mess," she said, turning around with cheeks flushed. She kept her eyes on the ground as she walked back over. "Have a seat," she said, waving to the couch.

"We're fine," Liam said.

"We wanted to ask you a few questions about Joseph Coulter," Mark began.

She jumped as though he had hit her. "Wh-what about him?" she asked.

"What was the nature of your relationship with him?"

"We were...friends," she said the word as though it were loathsome to her. She folded her arms over her chest, her body language clearly suggesting that she was hiding something.

"Were the two of you romantically involved while you worked at the charity?"

"We were," she bit her lip, fidgeted from foot to foot, "there was a lot of flirting, but we weren't a couple."

"Were you aware that he's getting married in a week?"

"Yes!" she hissed, and pure rage crossed her face. Mark forced himself not to take a step back or otherwise acknowledge her outburst.

"Look, what is this about? I'm very busy, and you'll have to go," she said.

Mark took a deep breath. "Actually, we were wondering if you knew a woman named Michaela, dark hair, she worked at the charity at the same time you did. She made a lot of threats against Joseph at the time, and we were hoping you might have witnessed some of them."

"Threats against Joseph?" she asked, her face draining of color. "Who would dare?"

"So, you didn't witness her threatening to kill him?"

"No! I wouldn't have just stood by if I had. Who is this woman? What's her last name?" she demanded.

"Unfortunately I can't say more than that at the moment." Mark pulled a card out of his pocket. "If you think of anything, please give me a call. We have reason to believe that she's trying to kill Joseph and we really need to find her."

She crushed the card in her fist. "Believe me, I'll keep an eye out for her," she said.

"Thanks, we appreciate the help," Mark said.

He was almost at the door when he turned back. "Is your new house as nice as this one?" he asked conversationally.

"No, I'm moving to an apartment," she said absently, staring off into space.

He turned and he and Liam left.

Once in the car Liam whistled low. "She is a piece of work. Just so I'm clear, there is no Michaela, right?"

"Right. I wanted to see how she'd react to a perceived threat to Joseph."

"You mean, other than from her?"

"Exactly. I'm pretty certain we can blame her for the attacks against Geanie, but I don't think she wants to hurt Joseph."

"Then how do you explain what happened with the tailors?" Liam asked.

"I can't explain it, at least, not yet. Hopefully something will come to me, though. One thing, at least, is clear."

"What's that?"

"We need to do some more digging on Amanda. I want you to pull up her financials and I'm going to put in a warrant to search her house. She's hiding something."

"Behind that closed door?"

"Exactly. And I plan to find out what it is."

They headed back toward the police station. Once inside they separated, hoping to get things moving on both tasks as quickly as possible. Before Mark could fill out the paperwork for the warrant, though, his phone rang.

"We've got a problem," Taylor, one of the other officers, told him. The man sounded out of breath.

Mark swore under his breath as he lurched up out of his chair. "Something happen up at the house?"

"No. It's about one of the bridesmaids."

12

Forty-five minutes later Mark arrived outside a condo in Los Angeles to find a frustrated Taylor. "What's going on?" he asked.

The man jerked his thumb at the front door. "Melissa, one of the bridesmaids, won't even let me in there. She flat out refused to come with me, said she won't leave the city for a whole week in case she gets calls for work. Apparently she's an aspiring actress."

"This is ridiculous," Mark said. He pounded on the door and it opened a crack. He held up his badge. "We're taking you into protective custody now," he said. "You've got ten minutes to grab whatever you need and then we're out of here."

"No," she said.

"Don't think I won't kick down this door and drag you out," he threatened, using his most menacing voice.

"You wouldn't dare!" she squeaked.

"Try me. The last thing I need with a killer running around is one more person exposed."

"I can't. I won't. What if I get a call?"

"*If* you get a call, we can cross that bridge when we get to it. I very much doubt it's going to be an issue, though. If you have a day job I can talk to your manager for you, explain what's happening here."

She shook her head furiously. "I-I didn't sign up for this...this drama."

He bit back a snide comment about how by trying to be an actress she had, indeed, signed up for drama. He took a deep breath. "Look, I need all the bridal party together where I can protect you."

"Then, count me out!"

"Of what?"

"Of the wedding!"

She slammed the door and Mark resisted the urge to kick it in just on principle.

"Some friend she is," he muttered to Taylor before pulling out his phone. He took a moment to try and calm himself down. He had thought telling Geanie that someone was trying to hurt her was hard. Telling her that one of her bridesmaids was abandoning her at the eleventh hour was going to be a thousand times worse. He toyed with calling Cindy and letting her be the one to break the bad news, but he knew that was the coward's way out.

Geanie picked up right away. "Detective, what is it?" she asked, her voice fearful.

"I have a bit of a situation here with your bridesmaid, Melissa."

"She doesn't want to come with you?" Geanie guessed.

"She refuses, actually. In fact, she seems to want out of the wedding altogether."

There was a moment of silence and then Geanie said, "Give her the phone," in a voice that he had never heard before.

He pounded on the door.

"Go away!"

"Phone, for you," Mark said.

The door opened and Melissa took the phone.

Mark wished he could just grab her and haul her off to the car, but despite his threats, he couldn't actually force her to go with him. She wasn't a suspect, nor a witness, and without an actual threat against her personally he couldn't even justify protective custody.

"Hello?" Melissa said.

He couldn't hear what Geanie said, but the hostility in her voice made even him wince.

"I can't be part of your crazy world with your whackadoodle friends and people trying to kill you. I have my own life, my own career to think about. You're asking too much of anyone."

There was another torrent from Geanie.

"No, I'm out. I'm not going to be a bridesmaid, and that's final," Melissa said.

Mark heard Geanie's next words crystal clear. "I won't forget this."

Melissa handed the phone back to Mark. Geanie had already hung up.

"There, you can leave me alone now," Melissa said defiantly.

"It's a shame," Mark said, pocketing his phone. "For someone obsessed with her career, you just made a big mistake."

"How do you figure?" she sneered.

Mark shook his head. "Clearly you're trying to make it on your looks and not your brains. Geanie is marrying a guy with more money than you could ever dream of who sits on the boards of some of the biggest charities in southern California alongside some of the biggest names in Hollywood. If you had played nice, he probably could have gotten you a starring role in any movie you wanted. Too bad you chose to throw that away," Mark said.

He turned and walked away.

When they reached the parking lot Taylor turned to him. "That was cold."

"It was also the truth. She pissed me off, especially that whole 'you're asking too much of anyone'. When you have a good friend, you go the extra mile for them and you never even worry about what's in it for you or what it might cost."

More times than he could count Paul had been there for him, going the extra mile. Whoever Paul had been, Mark knew without a shadow of a doubt, that the friendship had been real. Sometimes he just needed to stop and remind himself of that.

He turned with a sigh to Taylor. "Tell you what, go home. I'll pick up the other one."

"Are you sure?" Taylor asked.

"Yeah, I've got this. I'm just hoping she's less of a pain than this one."

Mark got into his car and typed Veronica's address into his GPS. She also lived in L.A., but on the outskirts headed toward Pine Springs.

He hit the road and a minute later Traci called.

"How's it going?" she asked.

"Crazy day," he said with a sigh.

"Any chance you'll take one day off this week?" she asked.

"It's not looking good. Why, what did you have in mind?" he asked.

"I just wanted to spend some time with my incredibly handsome husband."

He smiled. "I am so looking forward to that vacation you and I are going to be taking soon."

"You sound more stressed than you did this morning."

"One of Geanie's bridesmaids refused to come with us and stay at Joseph's for the next week. She actually told Geanie she wouldn't be a bridesmaid anymore."

"A week before the wedding?" Traci gasped.

"I know, how terrible is that? I mean, you would not have believed how psycho this girl was."

"Poor Geanie, she must be freaking out."

"Yeah, to find out your friend isn't your friend that way is harsh."

"And it creates a logistical nightmare for the wedding."

"How so?"

"Because now the bridesmaids and the groomsmen will be unequal."

Mark shook his head. He wouldn't have even thought about that. Then again, all he remembered of their wedding was how amazing Traci had looked and how her eyes had sparkled all night. He had been a babbling idiot, so excited and terrified half the time he couldn't even talk straight.

The GPS directed him off the freeway.

"Hon, I got to go. I'm about to get the other bridesmaid. Hopefully this one will be more cooperative," he said.

"Good luck."

"Thanks, I could use some of that right about now," he admitted.

Ten minutes later he was knocking on Veronica's door, hoping she was ready. He'd called both bridesmaids ahead of time and he was hoping this one hadn't also decided to change her mind.

The door opened and Veronica smiled at him. With her black circled eyes and black lipstick she reminded him strangely of the black rose. "I'm all set," she said.

"Great."

"I've got a lot of bags, though," she said, opening the door wide.

She had six of them to be exact. It took both of them two trips to get it all into his car. Then they headed off.

"This is so exciting," she gushed. "I'm part of a real, live murder investigation."

Mark wanted to slam his head into the steering wheel. A death-obsessed groupie was the last thing he needed.

"Exciting isn't the word I would choose," he said carefully.

"Maybe not, it's just, nothing cool ever happens to me. Geanie has told me so many stories about her roommate and I've always just wished I could be her, you know."

"Well, I'm sure Cindy would gladly trade places with you," he said.

His mind drifted back to the black rose. Cindy had been clear that the intruder who likely left it was a man. Maybe Sonja, the American assassin, wasn't the one they should be looking for. Then again, whoever the assassin was they'd already used at least two other people to do some of their dirty work so it was possible the black rose guy had just been another tool.

"What do you think?" Veronica asked.

"Sorry, about what?" Mark asked.

"Is law enforcement a good career choice?"

"It can be," he said, taking a deep breath. It was going to be a long car ride.

~

Jeremiah was back on the couch in the living room after having showered, shaved, and gotten dressed in clean clothes. He felt immeasurably better even if it did irritate him that he was being forced to lay on the couch while there were things that needed to be done.

Joseph had fallen asleep after eating and the others had all scattered to different parts of the mansion. The wedding planner had arrived, but Joseph had already been asleep so Cindy and Geanie had taken the woman upstairs to talk. He didn't know where Geanie's family had gone, but he suspected it was to their rooms. He could get up, but wasn't sure where he'd go. He couldn't leave, and he wasn't in any mood to just go to his room.

He couldn't stop thinking about the black rose. It wasn't the first time he'd seen one like that. Of course, the last time he'd seen one had been almost ten years before, in that other life, the one he could never share with Cindy.

He chafed with frustration. He had information, information that could help solve this case, but he couldn't share it with anyone, least of all Mark. Of course, even if he could tell him, it wouldn't matter. Pine Springs police, as good as they were, were no match for what was coming.

He had to do everything he could to rest up and prepare. He was going to need to make it back to his house for just a few minutes soon to get some supplies. Unless, of course, Joseph had an armory he hadn't bothered touring him through. There was no way for him to be able to effectively go on the offensive. So, instead he was just going to have to watch and wait, being even more vigilant than he normally was. He was getting tired of having to go it alone on so many things, though. Just once it would be nice to share with someone.

As if on cue Captain wandered into the room. The dog whined and licked his face. Jeremiah scratched behind his ears and smiled. "You missed me, even with all these friends to play with and having this huge place to roam?"

The dog licked him again before jumping up on the couch and settling down at Jeremiah's feet. He had no idea what Joseph's policy was about dogs on the furniture, but given how the other man doted on his own Jeremiah guessed it would be fine.

~

Cindy was relieved that Geanie was in a better mood than she had been after the call with Melissa. The wedding planner's stress over everything being 'unbalanced' hadn't helped. She was gone now, though, and it was just the two of them talking some more about Geanie's secret plans for the wedding.

"You guys love your secrets," Cindy finally teased.

"Yes, and no. Joseph and I tell each other everything. But, we both love surprises. Of course, sometimes even good surprises can cause a bit of stress."

"Still don't know where you're going on your honeymoon?" Cindy guessed.

"No, Joseph is being very cagey about that. He won't give up the secret."

"I think the two of you are trying to outdo each other with surprises," Cindy said with a smile.

"Yeah, it's just, his makes it hard to figure out how to pack."

"I think I can help with that one," Cindy said.

"Really?"

"Yeah, I've got you covered. I can tell you exactly what you should pack."

"Shoot."

"Lingerie."

"Yeah. What else?"

"Nope, that's it. Just lingerie," Cindy said with a smirk.

Geanie just gaped at her, apparently speechless.

"What? It's your honeymoon! What else are you going to need, really?"

"But, we're going to need clothes so we can go out."

"To do what?" Cindy asked.

"Eat, for starters."

"Oh, Geanie. That's what room service is for. And I'm sure Joseph would agree with me on this one."

"You're terrible!"

"Why? You've waited all your life for this, why not enjoy it to the fullest extent possible?"

Geanie giggled and turned red. "I see your point, but what if Joseph has made other plans, outdoor activities?"

"If he has, then he's not thinking straight. Tell you what, though, see if you can at least get him to tell you whether you should be packing for warm weather or cold."

"That's a brilliant idea!"

"I do occasionally have them."

Geanie leaned forward and hugged her. "Thank you for everything. I don't know how I could have handled any of this without you."

"You're welcome."

"Too bad you couldn't have talked as much sense into Melissa as you did my parents."

"Yeah, what was with them?" Cindy asked, unable to hide her bewilderment any longer.

"Ever since I moved out here my mother has been paranoid that I'd be swept off my feet by some smooth-talking guy who threw money around and would later break my heart. She's got that whole mistaken opinion that half of California is populated by smarmy Hollywood types and the other half is populated by hippies."

"I take it she's never been out for a visit?"

"Nope. When I told her I was dating she was paranoid, worried for me. When I finally told her that Joseph had money..."

"She thought all her dire predictions were coming true."

"Yeah. She just wouldn't hear what I had to say. I mean, for someone with his kind of money Joseph is the most opposite of the jet-setting crowd as he possibly could be."

"That's true."

"I knew that if they met him, gave him a chance, he'd win them over. I think you actually really got them to calm down. I think they just needed someone other than me to tell them things were okay."

"Glad I could help."

Cindy's phone rang and she answered it. A minute later she handed it to Geanie with a grin. "I think I just solved one of your other problems, too."

~

Liam called Mark halfway through the drive, a fact he was immeasurably grateful for.

"Found something interesting," the other detective said.

"What?"

"I pulled up Amanda's financial records. The house did indeed appear to close just recently. In fact, she deposited a check for just over half a million into her bank account."

"So, her story holds up so far."

"Yes, but here's where it gets interesting. A few days later she took out five hundred thousand. All in cash."

"Cash?"

"Yup. And, she told us she was moving into an apartment? Well, there's no record of any checks or credit card purchases made out to anything like that. No deposits, nothing. There haven't been any credit checks run in the last three months either."

"And apartments always run those before they let someone sign a lease. So, unless she's moving in with someone else, she's lying about moving into an apartment."

"Makes you wonder where she thinks she's going to go," Liam said.

"And what she's done with all that cash."

"I know you had to dash, so I submitted the paperwork to get the search warrant."

"What would I do without you?" Mark asked.

"Be a month behind in all your cases?" Liam teased.

Mark smiled to himself as he ended the call. He was really beginning to enjoy having Liam as a partner.

"Sounds like that was important," Veronica said, eyes wide.

"It was," Mark admitted.

He picked up the phone and tried calling Traci, wishing they could finish their conversation from earlier but also desperate to end the one with Veronica.

"Coming home yet?" Traci asked.

"No, I've got the second bridesmaid with me, though, and we're heading for Joseph's. I'll be there for a while. Then, unless I get the search warrant I want, I'll be heading home. You might as well have dinner without me. Either way it's going to be a long night."

"I'm not enjoying all this time apart," she said with a sigh.

"I know, but it can't be helped."

"All of your cases take up a lot of time, but this one seems especially time-intensive."

"Tell me about it, I feel that I've been living either at the hospital or at Joseph's. It's ridiculous."

"Well, I'm going to hold off in hopes of a late dinner. I miss you."

"I miss you, too," he said.

He hated the fact that right after finding out the biggest news of their lives it felt like they got no time together to marvel, to talk, to just be together before their lives changed forever. It wasn't fair. He was tired of asking her to put up with that kind of craziness.

"You're the best, you know that?" he asked.

"Oh, you have no idea," she said, and he could hear the smile in her voice.

He finally hung up as he exited the freeway near Joseph's house.

"Now, just so we're clear," he told Veronica. "You're going to be here for the next week. No side trips, no running out to get things. If, and only if, there is a pressing reason to leave you will be escorted by police officers. Is that clear?"

"Perfectly," she said, still looking excited.

He realized there was no way he was going to be able to impress upon her just how dangerous this whole situation really was, so he might as well stop trying. The truth was, as much as he wanted all the potential targets in one place because it was easier to concentrate the manpower to protect them, it was a huge gamble. He literally was putting all his eggs in one basket and if anything should upset that basket, they could all be killed in a moment. It was a risk they had to take, though. Hopefully the gamble would pay off.

They headed up the hill to Joseph's and he waved at the officers he could see as he parked in front of the house. Cindy came out and helped grab a couple of Veronica's bags from the trunk.

"How are the patients?" he asked.

"Restless, but behaving."

"Can't ask for any more than that," he muttered.

He followed her into the entryway, a bag in each hand. Geanie walked in from the kitchen just as a woman started down the stairs wearing a green dress.

Mark looked up and his jaw dropped as the bags slipped out of his hands. He turned on Cindy. "What is she doing here?" he demanded.

13

"She volunteered to replace Melissa as a bridesmaid," Cindy said with a grin.

"And I figured this would allow me to spend more time with my husband, so I figured I'd kill two birds with one stone," Traci said as she made it to the bottom of the stairs. She was wearing a forest green gown made out of satin that looked like a bridesmaid dress. "And don't worry, the neighbors are watching Buster."

"Although we did tell her that she could bring him," Cindy said.

Mark was dumbfounded. He'd never guessed Traci would go and do something like this.

"Well, aren't you going to say something?" Traci teased. She did a slow turn. "At least tell me how I look. It turns out Melissa and I wear the same size."

"Can I talk to you...outside," he said, unable to mask the stress in his voice.

"Sure," she said, her smile faltering slightly.

They walked outside and Mark closed the door behind them. Then they walked a few more steps before he turned to her. "Are you crazy? What are you doing?"

"I'm helping out," she said, crossing her arms and arching an eyebrow, a sure sign that she was settling in for a debate.

"You can't be here. This is the middle of a murder investigation."

"It's also the middle of a wedding, and my friends needed me."

"Geanie and you barely know each other!"

"We know each other well enough and she was thrilled when I volunteered."

"You volunteered!" he exploded. Until that moment he had been sure that Cindy had been the one to talk her into something so crazy.

"Of course I did. When I heard what happened, I couldn't leave them high and dry, could I?"

"Oh, so you're saying this is my fault? If I hadn't told you about that idiot wanna-be actress you wouldn't even be here?"

"I never said that, but if you want to look at it that way," she shrugged. Her eyes were sparking fire and any other day if he had seen that he would have quickly backed down. Not today, though, not over this.

Out of the corner of his eyes he saw the other officers retreat, clearly not wanting to be anywhere near this fight.

"What is your problem?" Traci demanded.

"My problem? My problem is that it's too dangerous to be here!"

"It can't be that dangerous or you wouldn't have risked the lives of your friends."

"I had no choice but to risk their lives. Their lives were already at risk before I even got here! This whole thing is one big gamble. I'm betting their lives on the fact that hopefully I didn't just make it easier for the killer to blow them all up at once!"

"Still, you have to be pretty confident," she said, hesitating ever so slightly.

"As confident as a man standing in a dynamite factory with a lit match," he said. "This thing could blow up in my face at any moment. But what else can I do? I'm certainly not comfortable putting my wife, my *pregnant* wife, into this situation."

"It's a good thing it's not up to you, then," she said softly.

He stared at her slack-jawed.

"Listen, Mark. You can't forbid me. We both know that won't work. I want to do this. Yes, I want to help out and I want to see more of you than I'm going to, but you have to remember, I'm going through a lot of changes."

"That's why I need to know you're safe," he pleaded.

"And I feel safer here, surrounded by people I care about than I do at home by myself."

"But what if something bad happens?" he whispered.

"Then, you'll protect me, just like you always do. And, let's be honest, the only times bad things have really happened to me have been when you've left me alone," she said.

She wasn't wrong, that's what killed him.

"And given my current state I wasn't particularly in the mood to be left alone. Besides, with all the police you're going to have sitting on this place, this should be the safest house in the state. If I were you I'd actually start worrying more about what you're going to do to secure the wedding and reception sites."

He snapped his mouth shut before he could say anything else. He'd been putting off thinking about securing those sites because he'd been hoping beyond hope they'd catch the killer before then. She was right, though. At the rate they were going the killer would still be at large next Saturday and they needed to have started planning for that contingency days before.

"You hate it when I'm right, don't you?" she said, a smile quirking the corners of her mouth.

"You know I do," he admitted.

"So, first, tell me how I look in my dress," she said, twirling again.

"Like an angel," he said, smiling grudgingly.

"Thank you. Now we can get down to the business of figuring out how to make this wedding safer than the real Royal Wedding was."

"Sometimes it scares me how smart you are," he said.

"I know. It's why we stopped playing Monopoly ages ago," she said with a grin.

He sighed. "I'm hoping you brought everything with you that you're going to need for this three hour tour?"

"Oh, enough for two weeks at least. Longer if I can get at a washing machine."

He held out his arm and she took it. "In that case, I'd better escort a certain bridesmaid back inside."

"You'd better. Rumor has it groomsmen are showing up shortly and I wouldn't want to have to wait for one of them to escort me inside."

"If Wildman lays one finger on you, I'll rip it off," Mark growled.

Her laughter pealed out across the lawns and it made everything else worth it.

~

"Everything okay?" Cindy asked, eyeing Traci and Mark as they came back inside. The couple were both smiling now, which was a good sign.

"Glorious," Mark said. "As it turns out, looks like I'll be staying the week, too."

"The more the merrier," Joseph said from the living room doorway.

"What are you doing up?" Mark barked at him.

"Heading to the restroom. And nothing on this earth can stop me," Joseph said, setting his jaw.

"Fine, just use one of the ones on this level, no climbing the stairs," Mark said.

Joseph grumbled something but Cindy couldn't quite make it out.

"Can I get the rest of my bags?" Veronica asked.

"Sure, knock yourself out," Mark said.

"I'll help you," Cindy said.

After they had brought in the rest of Veronica's luggage, Cindy helped her carry it upstairs. Veronica's room was next door to Charlotte's. Traci and Mark's was across the hall and next door to Milt and Dorothy's. That left three more guest rooms in that wing, one each for Dave and Jordan whenever they arrived, and one for the final groomsman who was flying in on Tuesday.

Cindy left Veronica to settle into her room and hurried back downstairs. She found everyone else gathered in the living room where Geanie was on her cell ordering pizza for everyone. She hung up at last. "There, food for twelve people."

"Come Tuesday when Lyle flies in it will be thirteen," Joseph commented.

"Quite a houseful," Mark commented. "Hope no one is overly superstitious."

Geanie rolled her eyes. "Please, this is a good thing. Thirteen is my favorite number."

"It always has been," Dorothy affirmed.

"Ever since she was little she had to be different than everyone else," Milt said with a laugh.

"What can I say? Normal is boring," Geanie said with a laugh.

"That, ladies and gentlemen, is my fiancée," Joseph said.

The pizza dinner ended up having a downright festive feel. It didn't take long afterward, however, for people to start yawning. It had been an exhausting day for all of them.

After Joseph fell asleep on his couch Cindy, Jeremiah, and Mark moved into the kitchen. She noticed that the detective only rolled his eyes slightly in Jeremiah's direction. He probably realized that trying to keep him on the couch was a losing battle.

Mark filled them in on everything he had learned from Gretchen about Paul. He also told them about his and Liam's visit to see Amanda. They both agreed that everything about her seemed incredibly suspicious.

"What about the rose, anything about that?" Jeremiah finally asked.

"Not yet. Probably won't hear anything back from forensics until Monday morning I'm guessing," Mark said, sounding irritated.

"I can't believe tomorrow's Sunday already," Cindy muttered.

"I can't believe that Marie knew I had an accident that was bad enough to get a replacement rabbi for services today, and I still haven't heard anything from her," Jeremiah said. "Usually she would have called and given me an earful by now."

"I told her we were putting you in police protection and no contact with the outside world. You're welcome," Mark said with a wink.

Jeremiah smiled. "It might be even worth the third degree she'll give me when this is all done."

"At least you have a small respite. Sometimes I get the impression she thinks of herself more as your mother than your secretary."

Jeremiah chuckled.

Cindy managed not to say anything. The number of dirty looks she got from Marie had not endeared the other woman to her.

"Okay, run me through the schedule for the rest of the week," Mark said.

"Tomorrow Joseph was going to throw a big barbeque for close friends and Geanie's family."

"Consider it canceled," Mark said. "Make sure to make the phone calls."

"I'll get right on that," Cindy said, unable to hide the sarcasm from her tone.

Mark looked questioningly at her. She just shook her head. She was tired, but he was right, Geanie had too much on her plate to worry about making those calls. She could handle it.

"Monday's a holiday," Jeremiah said. "There were plans to take Geanie's family and the bridal party to The Zone theme park."

"Also canceled, obviously," Mark said.

"Tuesday is the last meeting with the wedding planner, which can happen here," Cindy said.

"Good."

"Wednesday night was last minute running around and errands."

"Which, if they are absolutely necessary, someone else can handle. We'll talk about that later."

"Thursday night are the bachelor and bachelorette parties," Jeremiah said.

"Correction, 'were' the parties. Next?"

"Hold on," Cindy said.

"What?" Mark asked.

Cindy took a deep breath. "I know there's a killer on the loose and all kinds of craziness going on, but I refuse to let that ruin what should be the most special time in their lives. There's no way I want Geanie to look back and think, 'I wish I could have had a bachelorette party and a normal wedding.' She's only getting married once."

"I agree," Jeremiah said quietly.

"You two are crazier than Traci," Mark said. "Look, unless it can be done from the safety of the mansion, there is no way you can have those parties."

Cindy felt herself beginning to smile.

"What? I don't like that look," Mark said.

"It's settled," she said. "We'll have the parties here."

He groaned. "I know I'm going to live to regret saying that."

"If we're smart, we could even use them to set a trap for the killer," Jeremiah said. "If it worked, then things would be all clear for the wedding."

"And if it doesn't work the three of us are going to have words," Mark warned.

"Okay, we'll talk logistics in the morning," Cindy said. "Let's keep going. Friday all day we'll be decorating the reception site."

"The event planner should be taking care of that, right?"

"Not all of it. There are several little surprise touches Geanie is adding personally."

"I could forbid it."

"And I could talk to Traci," Cindy said smugly.

Mark sighed. "And?"

"Friday night is the rehearsal and the rehearsal dinner. The dinner's happening at Rue de Main."

Mark shook his head. "I'll be seeing a lot of that restaurant this month." He cleared his throat. "Then Saturday's the wedding and that's it, yes?"

"Yes," Cindy and Jeremiah chorused.

"Great, it's going to take every cop in Pine Springs and then some to pull this whole thing off," Mark sighed. "The captain is going to just love this."

"Don't forget, you've got a secret weapon on your side," Cindy said.

"Yeah, and just what would that be?" he asked.

"Us," Jeremiah answered.

~

Jeremiah couldn't sleep. He was in his room at the mansion, having refused to spend the night downstairs on

163

the couch. Captain was snoring away on the foot of the bed, unbothered by his master's insomnia.

His mind kept going back over everything again and again. Something felt off to him. He was missing a piece of the puzzle, and it was keeping him from even being able to see the picture clearly enough to know what it was that he was missing. It was making him crazy.

On top of that he was mentally reviewing the events of the coming week, going over and over them trying to figure out when and how the killer would strike next. The schedule wasn't exactly a secret. Dozens of people knew what the general plan for the next few days was--everyone from friends to vendors. The trick would be mixing it up just enough to keep the killer off balance. The more the killer had to improvise, the better their chances of stopping him or her.

He was too tired to think clearly enough to start to build a workable plan. In the morning, though, he'd sit down with Cindy and Mark and start to work something out. He had thought of having Joseph hire extra security, but at this point the last thing they needed were strangers running around the property. All the police officers were known to Mark, and, at this point, most of them Jeremiah knew as well, at least, on sight.

With a weary sigh he flipped over on his side and tried to go to sleep.

~

Mark woke up as he felt Traci get out of bed. "Everything okay?"

"Yes, I just drank way too much water with dinner," she said. "It turns out it takes three times the water to cut the spice of pepperoni as it does soda."

"I'm sorry. I know you're going to really miss your caffeine."

"It's worth it," she said as she moved toward the bathroom. "Besides, it's not like I have to give it up forever."

"True."

He propped himself up on one elbow. "I have to say, this has got to be one of the most comfortable mattresses I've ever slept on."

"I know. We have to figure out what kind it is so I can get one. The last few nights I've been waking up with pain in my back. I would have slept all night on this one if it weren't for all that water."

"Maybe if we ask nice Joseph will get us one as an early baby present," Mark joked.

"Ha ha, very funny. You're supposed to give presents that will help the baby."

"Making sure mommy sleeps well *will* help the baby," he said.

"Hilarious."

"Can't blame a guy for trying."

He laid back down and instantly his mind began to drift. It really was a very comfortable bed. This was going to be the best night sleep he'd had in who knew how long. He could feel the stress of the day melting away along with fears of hired killers and crazy stalkers. Everything was going to be okay. It had to be.

He heard the sound of the sink as Traci washed her hands but it sounded so far away. Had he told her he'd loved her yet today? He'd have to tell her when she came back to bed. He--

Mark bolted out of bed, instantly wide awake, as Traci let out a piercing scream.

14

Three seconds later Mark was in the bathroom flipping on the light. "What is it?"

"Something, something touched my arm," Traci said, her voice shaking.

"There's no one here but us," Mark said.

"Not someone. Some*thing*."

Mark looked around. There was a wide-brimmed drinking glass on the counter next to their toothbrushes. A toiletry bag sat behind that. On the other end of the counter was a gift bag with tissue paper sticking out the top. laying on its side. Near that was a hand towel.

"What did it feel like?" he asked as he dropped his eyes to the ground.

"It was big, not like a fly, bigger, like a lizard maybe."

"Where were you when it touched you?"

"Here, I was standing right here. I had just washed my hands and I was about to dry them on this towel," she said, pointing to the hand towel.

He leaned around the edge of the counter to look at the area of floor between the cabinets and the toilet and that was when he saw it.

It was a snake, its body curled up in a figure eight with its head in the center. He was a grayish color with white spots edged with brown.

"Traci, walk into the other room," Mark said. It took all his willpower to keep his voice calm and neutral.

She did as instructed instantly, without question. Mark kept his eyes on the snake. He heard a pounding on the bedroom door. He heard Traci open the door. Someone was inquiring about her scream. A moment later someone joined him in the bathroom.

"What is it?"

He was momentarily surprised to hear Wildman's voice instead of Jeremiah's. It made sense, though, Jeremiah was in an entirely different wing of the house and Wildman was just a couple of doors down.

"Snake, next to the toilet," Mark said, trying to back up slowly.

Wildman moved cautiously, craning his head until he could see, then he backed out of the bathroom. "Do you have your gun?" he asked, voice strained.

"Of course, why?"

"Can you hit that thing with one shot?" the youth pastor asked.

"Yes, why?"

"For heaven's sake, tell me where the gun is, because you need to kill that snake before it can bite anyone."

Normally Mark would never have let the other man go get his gun, but he was behind him and the sound in his voice struck more terror into Mark's heart than he had ever known.

"End table, right side of the bed. Careful, it's loaded."

Seconds later the youth pastor handed him his gun. Mark grabbed it without taking his eyes off the snake.

"You have to kill it."

"I understand," Mark said, his mouth completely dry. He took careful aim, let out his breath, focused, and squeezed the trigger.

In the confines of the bathroom the sound of the gun going off was deafening, so loud that it even startled Mark. The snake jerked and for one horrific moment Mark thought he had missed. Then he spotted the hole in the animal's head and he sagged against the doorjamb. He realized he had started shaking.

He could hear shouts and pounding steps coming from several directions now.

Traci met everyone at the door, informing people as they arrived that Mark had shot a snake in the bathroom. The news seemed to be causing a great deal of bewilderment out in the hall, but not nearly as much as he was feeling from where he was.

A minute later Jeremiah showed up. Apparently Traci had let him through. He glanced in and saw the body of the snake and then turned to Mark, a questioning look on his face.

"Traci got up to use the bathroom. She screamed because she thought something touched her arm when she was going to dry her hands. She must have knocked it on the floor. Wildman here showed up and told me I had to shoot it."

"Good call," Jeremiah said grimly.

He moved over to Traci and Mark watched out of the corner of his eye as she and Jeremiah double checked her arms for signs of bite marks.

"She's okay," Jeremiah called after a moment.

Mark turned finally at that, realizing suddenly that he still had the gun in his hand. He walked back over and put it back away in the end table. He looked at the youth pastor who was now sitting on the edge of the bed, face white, hands clasped together as if he were praying.

He and the other groomsman had arrived after dinner just before almost everyone turned in. There hadn't really been more than a chance to say hello. Mark sat down next to him now, his knees feeling weak as the adrenalin started to leave his body.

"What, what kind of snake was it?" Mark asked.

"A saw-scaled viper, a young one, not yet fully grown."

"I take it they're poisonous?"

"One of the deadliest snakes in the world."

"I wonder how it got in here?" Mark said. "I mean, I guess it's possible it came in through the pipes or something."

Dave shook his head. "You don't understand. That snake didn't just happen in here. They're only found in the middle east and parts of Asia, including India."

The middle east. Two of the possible assassins that Liam's contacts had come up with were from that region. Mark felt a chill dance down his spine. He had been betting on the American assassin, but it looked like he might be wrong.

"How did you know I needed to shoot it then?" Mark asked.

"I took a mission trip to Bangladesh a couple of years ago. I saw a man bit by one. It didn't end well."

"I'm glad you were here," Mark said.

Dave nodded.

The two of them just sat there, Mark didn't know for how long. It was a toss-up which one of them was more deeply in shock than the other. Mark should be doing something, securing the room, figuring out where the snake came from, how the assassin got him in the house. Instead all he did, all he felt like he could do, was sit next to Dave and stare into space.

A crime scene investigator showed up and at some point, took some pictures, and removed the snake. Mark and Dave just continued to sit. Maybe this was what having a mental breakdown felt like, Mark thought at last.

A few minutes later Traci touched his shoulder. "Honey, you should try and get some sleep."

It was funny, the fact that she thought he could sleep given that she had just nearly been killed by a poisonous snake from halfway around the world that had somehow ended up in their bathroom.

He blinked. Why their bathroom? If the assassin had left the snake when he broke in wouldn't he have chosen a room that was occupied, or at least one near where people would be? This entire wing had been empty at the time. The snake could have easily gone undiscovered until well after the wedding. At that point it would have been more likely found by some sort of maid than anyone else.

What if the assassin hadn't left it himself, but had had it smuggled in?

He turned and looked at Traci who looked very tired but even more concerned. "When you came over here earlier today, did you drive straight here from our house?" he asked.

She frowned. "No, I stopped at the pharmacy first. I needed more anti-nausea medicine."

"How long were you inside?"

"Five minutes, maybe ten. There was a pretty long line."

Mark stood up abruptly and went back into the bathroom. He took another look at the things on the counter, where the snake had touched her.

"What's in this gift bag in here?" he called.

Traci appeared beside him in the doorway. "A bunch of funny little stuff, it's for Geanie's bachelorette party."

"So, this is a present for her?"

"Yes."

"Where was it in the car when you were at the pharmacy?"

"It was on the passenger seat. I didn't want it getting squished by the bags, there's a little glass bottle in there."

"Why is it in the bathroom?"

"Because right before I went to bed I couldn't find where I packed my travel mouthwash. I finally went and got the bag, because I had one in there for Geanie. Fortunately it was on top so I didn't have to go rummaging for it. I figured when I found mine later I'd just switch them out. They're the same brand and both of them are brand new. Why?"

"Because I think while you were at the store someone slipped that snake into that gift bag, hoping that it would bite Geanie when she opened it."

Traci backed up until she ran into the bed and then she sat down abruptly next to Dave. "Are you serious?" she whispered.

"Yes. I told you, this is all very dangerous," he said.

"You mean, I almost got Geanie killed because I didn't want to spend an hour each day throwing up?"

"No, you almost got yourself killed," he corrected.

"What kind of lunatic does something like this?"

"A highly paid one, I imagine," he said grimly.

"Mark, you have to find him and stop him."

"I've been doing my best, honey," he said, softening his voice. "It will be okay, you'll see."

"How did he know? How did he know to follow me, that I would be coming here and everything?"

"I don't know. It could have been a lucky guess based on my movements. We'll have to figure that out," he said.

Personally he was wondering if their assassin had tapped someone's phone.

"We're not going to solve anything else right now," Jeremiah said quietly.

Mark looked up. He'd forgotten that the rabbi was still there. "We can have the rest of your luggage checked out in the morning. I'm sure there's another room we can move you to for tonight," he said.

Mark shook his head slowly. "The snake was meant for Geanie, I'm sure of it. Besides, I was all through our other bags earlier trying to figure out where Traci packed my pajamas. If there was a snake in any of them I'd be dead by now."

The words sounded good, but in truth he wasn't sure he was feeling that brave. There was a hole in the bathroom where a while before a deadly snake had been. He winced at the thought.

"I doubt Joseph's home insurance covers bullet holes," he muttered darkly.

"What did you say?" Jeremiah asked.

"Nothing. It was a bad joke. You're right, though. I don't think there's anything more that can be done tonight."

~

Long after the others had turned in for the second time that night Jeremiah paced the halls of the mansion. He walked silently, passing within inches of people's doors without a sound. As he paced he thought and the most important thing he was trying to decide was just how paranoid he was.

The rose and the snake had both been clear messages. Each deeply symbolic.

The rose symbolized so many things: love, purity, friendship, union. One stripped of its flowers and containing only thorns had a much harsher message, the absence of those things. A black rose itself had been used as a symbol for various things such as Irish nationalism and anarchy. The most plain and ordinary meaning, though, was death, particularly the death of love.

Given that there was a wedding that was being interrupted that made perfect sense. However, he was becoming less sure that the rose had been a reference to Geanie and Joseph and a disrupted union. The introduction of the serpent as a symbol had solidified that in his mind.

The serpent was a symbol of evil, of corruption, sin. Not just any sin, either, but original sin. It had been the creature used to tempt Eve in the Garden to eat of the tree of the Knowledge of Good and Evil. He couldn't help but feel that there was a message there, and that it was sent by the same person who had sent the note to Mark which read 'Ask him what his name is'.

Mark's wife had been used to carry the snake and to unwittingly introduce it into his life. And Mark was most certainly after knowledge.

Ask him what his name is.

And regardless of who the 'him' in the message turned out to be, good and evil were at the heart of the knowledge that Mark was seeking. Obtaining that knowledge had ultimately doomed Adam and Eve to death. He could only pray that Mark's quest for knowledge would not have the same result.

He tried to tell himself that he was reading too much into these things, but something in his gut wouldn't let it all go. He was on the right track, he could feel it, but he didn't know what he could do about it, not without putting the others in more danger than they were already in.

The whole thing was a nightmare and it was being complicated by too many players on the board. There were far too many variables, too many people to watch and to watch out for. Disaster was in the air and he wasn't sure that this time he would be able to avert it.

~

Sunday morning Cindy rose early. It was even too early really to call Gerald. She wandered downstairs, figuring she'd check on Joseph. He was still asleep on the couch in the living room. She was glad, he needed his rest, especially with everything that had happened and whatever insanity lay ahead of them.

She made her way into the kitchen and was startled to see Mark sitting at the breakfast bar, sipping a cup of coffee.

"Morning," he said.

"Good morning. Did you sleep at all?"

"Off and on," he admitted. "You're up early."

"Yeah, well," she shrugged. "I'm guessing church this morning is out of the question?"

"I won't even dignify that with an answer," he said.

"That's what I thought," she said with a sigh.

She went over to the far counter and checked out Joseph's tea selections. "Does this actually say 'chocolate tea'?" she asked after a moment.

"Beats me, I went straight for the coffee."

"Well, I'm going to have to give this a try."

"Sounds like the breakfast of champions," he said drily.

"Let's hope so," she said.

Five minutes later she sat down on a stool next to him, holding her mug.

"It certainly smells chocolaty," Mark commented.

"I know," she said. She took a small sip. "Tastes that way, too. You know, I kind of like it."

They sat for another minute in silence before Cindy asked, "So, are you ready to discuss details yet?"

He shook his head. "I'm still half-dead. I'm not sure I'd even remember half of what we talked about. Besides, I want to wait for the rabbi. He's usually got a unique perspective on things."

"He does, doesn't he," she mused. She took another sip of her tea. "What do you think his story is?"

"I don't want to know and if I don't want to know, I'm doubly sure you don't want to know," Mark said brusquely.

"Trust me on this one, I'd let it alone if I were you. What is it they say? The truth is a double-edged sword."

"I guess you're right," Cindy said with a sigh. To be honest she wasn't even sure what had possessed her to ask Mark about Jeremiah. Maybe she was just looking for someone else's insight or reassurance. She shook her head. She was tired, more tired than she had realized.

Clearly Mark was, too. At this rate they were all going to be the walking dead by the time Saturday rolled around. She just prayed this whole thing would be over soon so they could relax and get some rest before then.

Her phone rang and she saw that it was Gerald. Surprised that he would be calling this early she hastily answered. "Hi, I was planning on calling you a little later," she said.

"What I have to say couldn't wait," he said, his voice strained.

"Why, what did you find out?" she asked.

"You better sit down."

"I am sitting down."

"Good, because you are not going to believe what I just found out."

"Tell me," she said, breathlessly.

"Okay, I did some digging and I followed a lead down to New Orleans. Matthew is-"

Gerald shouted, she heard a crash and then the line went dead.

15

"Gerald? Gerald!" Cindy was shouting into her phone.

Mark felt himself come fully awake as he stared at the horrified expression on her face. She tried calling the man back but he could hear the voicemail pick up.

"Please, Gerald, call me back. Let me know you're okay," Cindy pleaded.

Finally she put her phone down on the breakfast bar and stared at it as though she could will it to ring.

"What happened?" Mark asked quietly.

"Something terrible," Cindy whispered, sounding heartbroken.

"Look at me," he said sharply.

She did as she was told.

"Tell me what just happened," he demanded.

"He said he found out something about Matthew that I wasn't going to believe. He followed a lead to New Orleans. I think he might have actually gone there, I don't know. He said I wasn't going to believe what he had to say. He said 'Matthew is' and then he shouted and there was a crash before the line went dead."

"Matthew is...what?"

"I don't know," she said, her eyes tearing up. "And what if the answer to that just got him killed?"

"But why, by who?"

"There has to be something we can do," she said. "I got him involved in all of this. I asked him to help."

"He was already involved. He wrote about that cult and whatever questions he was asking were reason enough for Paul to threaten him. Something is going on here that is bigger than we think it is. This can't all be about keeping the past buried, especially since that mass grave has been found."

"But-"

"No, whatever is going on is not your fault. Look, I'll put a call in to the New Orleans police and see if they know anything, and ask them to notify me if anything comes up."

"Thank you," she whispered.

"Hey, it's the least I can do. And besides, if anyone is responsible for getting him into whatever mess he's in, it's me. I'm the one who asked for help from anyone and everyone figuring out the whole Paul thing. Believe me, if I could put an end to all that I would in a heartbeat."

"The truth will come out, I'm sure of it," she said.

"I hope so, for all our sakes," he said grimly. "Now, give me a few minutes, I have to make some calls."

She nodded, grabbed her tea and her phone and left the kitchen.

~

Cindy sat in a chair in the living room, quietly sipping her tea and trying not to freak out. When she'd walked in the room she'd had a momentarily insane thought of waking Joseph and asking to borrow money for airfare to New Orleans. The thought was short-lived, though, as she realized she wouldn't even know where to begin when she got there and she could search for weeks and still not find Gerald or anything about him.

Plus, there was no way she could abandon everyone here. Whatever was happening to Gerald was happening now. There was nothing she could do to stop it or help. On the other hand, there were people here and now who she could help.

Why did life have to be so complicated? Why did she have to choose which of her friends to try and help? The longer she sat there, spending too much time alone in her own head, the worse she felt.

It was with relief that she waved silently at Geanie as she entered the room. Geanie waved back and then went to look at Joseph who was still sleeping. She turned finally and came to sit down in the chair right next to Cindy.

"Good morning," Geanie whispered.

"Morning," Cindy said, forcing a smile for the other woman's sake. Geanie had enough stress of her own without adding Cindy's to it.

"I wonder what surprises today will bring?"

"I don't know, but Mark nixed the barbeque for this afternoon."

"I heard. I'll have to make some calls."

"I can do that," Cindy said. It would give her something to do.

"Joseph's going to be disappointed."

"We could always have a barbeque just with the people here," Cindy said. "After all, there's enough of us that it will still be pretty lively."

"That's a good idea," Geanie said, perking up.

180

"We could even play croquet. I mean, we're stuck here, but we don't necessarily have to be stuck inside. The whole mountain is under guard, after all."

"Do you think Mark will object?"

"Probably, but I bet I can make a good argument," Cindy said with a smile. At the very least, she could sic Traci on him. She knew that woman could be persuasive.

"Did someone say barbeque?" Joseph asked groggily.

"Yes, now go back to sleep," Geanie whispered.

"Not a chance. I've slept too much," Joseph said, struggling to sit up. Once he had achieved that he yawned and stretched.

"You know what?" he said at last.

"What?" Cindy asked.

"I'm going to go take a shower and get into some clean clothes and no one can stop me."

"I don't think anyone other than Mark will object," Cindy said.

"And Cindy's already working on ways to make him see reason," Geanie said, moving to sit over next to Joseph.

"Great," he said, giving her a quick kiss. "Now, if you ladies will excuse me, I need to go get cleaned up so I can feel like a new man. Or, at least, a less abused man."

As soon as he'd left Cindy turned back to Geanie. "There's something I've been meaning to talk to you about. I was hesitant to bring it up, but it occurs to me that if I wait any longer it will be too late."

"What is it?" Geanie asked, looking concerned.

"What are you planning to do about your wedding dress?" Cindy asked, wincing even as she said it.

The second dress, the one Geanie had been wearing when the bridal shop exploded, had been singed beyond repair. If they were going to have to find a new dress they were going to have to get one of the police officers to take them shopping as soon as possible. Even still, it would be cutting things painfully close.

"I've been thinking about that," Geanie said. "I think I've decided that the smartest choice is to go with the first dress."

"You mean the one Joseph's seen?" Cindy asked, surprised.

"He swears that all he saw was the faintest peep of white satin, which, hello, isn't really that much of a surprise. I mean, sure I could have gone for something covered in lace, or broken with tradition and worn some other color, but really, that wasn't going to happen. So, as long as all he knows is that it's white satin, I think I can live with that."

"I think that's probably a smart choice," Cindy said.

Geanie nodded. "The dress is here, it's safe, no other businesses or people will be harmed by my making the choice to stick with what I've got."

"And it really does look amazing, even more you than the second one."

"Yeah, I'm just sorry there's no way to repair that second one. It would have made a great wedding dress for you someday."

Cindy blushed, but didn't argue with her.

"Plus, everything else I've got already works with that dress," Geanie said. "It's the logical choice given... everything."

"I think it's the right choice regardless of everything," Cindy said with an encouraging smile.

"Thanks."

"So, has Joseph given you any hint yet as to what kind of clothes to pack for the honeymoon?"

"That man is impossible," Geanie said with a roll of her eyes. "All he'd tell me was that I should pack one suitcase for warm weather and one suitcase for cold."

"That's not even a little helpful."

"I know, right?"

"What are you ladies talking about?" Jeremiah asked as he walked into the room, making them both jump slightly.

"Honeymoons," Geanie said brightly.

"Ah."

"Has Joseph told you where he's planning on taking her?" Cindy asked.

Jeremiah smiled sheepishly. "Yes, and at the same time, no."

"Okay. Can you at least tell us if she should pack for warm or cold weather?"

"No, I really can't. What did Joseph say?"

"Pack a bag of each."

He laughed. "That...makes sense."

"Okay, tell us what you know," Cindy demanded.

"I'm sorry, I was told to treat this like a state secret. These lips are sealed," Jeremiah said.

"Go over there and see if you can unseal them," Geanie whispered roguishly.

Cindy felt herself turn scarlet, but she didn't dignify the suggestion with a response. Instead she changed the subject. "I heard from Gerald, and I think he's in trouble."

"What happened?" Jeremiah asked.

Cindy filled him in and at the end of her story he was nodding. "It sounds like he probably is in trouble. He knows how to handle himself, though. Hopefully everything will set itself right."

"I wish I had your optimism," she grumbled.

~

Jeremiah forced a smile. At the moment he was far from optimistic about anything so what Cindy said seemed funny to him.

"I did want to get a few things straightened out about Thursday," he said.

"Bachelor and Bachelorette parties?" Cindy asked.

"Exactly."

"I don't want to know," Geanie said with a laugh as she stood up. "I'll leave you two to scheme."

"I had planned a night out at an old-fashioned vaudeville show," Jeremiah said. "How about you?"

"Vegas," Cindy said with a straight face.

"Are you kidding?" he blinked. "I mean, I know it's about five hours away, but still."

"Relax," she said with a grin. "Lingerie party and crazy games. Although, I'm beginning to think Geanie doesn't need any more lingerie. Clothes, maybe, but lingerie she seems to have covered."

"I don't need to know. I don't want to know," Jeremiah said. "Obviously, though, there has to be some rethinking of all of this, especially since both parties are going to be happening simultaneously and they now have to be happening here."

"So, you want to stake out territory?"

"Something like that."

"Okay, what did you have in mind?"

"I was thinking the guys could take over the basement area with the movie theater and the pool table and all of that."

"You know, I still haven't even been down there," Cindy said with a sigh.

"It's pretty amazing."

"Okay, but we get the formal living room and the formal dining room, and you have to help me rearrange furniture before the event."

"Done," he said.

"Well, that was easy."

"Maybe for you. The plans for your party didn't change, just the location. I have to rethink the whole thing."

"Why don't you get the vaudeville group to come here?"

He shook his head. "I thought about it, but we hadn't sold out the theater, so there will be other patrons there. Plus, there's no way Mark would let that many strangers into the house two days before the wedding. And rightly so," he added hastily at the end.

"Need some help brainstorming?"

He grinned. "Not that I don't value your opinion, but I think I want to talk to another guy about this. I'm thinking Dave and I can work something out between the two of us."

"I don't know, I think you're missing out on a fabulous opportunity," she teased. "I could have helped you throw Joseph a gothic high tea or something equally creative."

Jeremiah couldn't help it. He started laughing. "Creative? Yes. Manly? No."

"I bet Joseph would have liked my idea," she said.

"Are you kidding? Joseph's going to be thrilled with anything as long as there are no strippers or anything of that nature," Jeremiah said. "Not that I would have done anything like that, but he made it painfully clear anyway."

"I knew he was a good man," Cindy said with a grin.

"I think this will work out fine. We should be able to salvage both parties and make them memorable, in a good way."

"Isn't that what a wedding is all about? Getting the bride and groom married off with a bunch of happy memories to start their life together."

"I guess it is at that."

He stood up. "I'm going to make sure the dogs get their breakfast and then I'm thinking it's time we humans got ours."

"Sounds good. I'll meet you in the kitchen in a few minutes," she said.

"Works for me. Everyone will probably be getting up soon."

Jeremiah left the room, his mind whirring. It seemed ridiculous with everything that was going on to be fretting about the bachelor party, but he did care. He liked what Cindy had said about a bunch of good memories to start a life off together. That's what Joseph and Geanie deserved and he was going to do what he could to see that they got it.

Of course, he was going to have to get creative. He hoped that Wildman and he could come up with something fun to do. Of course, Wildman was used to planning activities for high school boys and not grown men. Deep down, though, there were fewer differences between the two groups than most liked to admit. The thought made him smile.

~

It took about half an hour but Mark finally got through to someone on the New Orleans police force who could help him. As it turned out they hadn't heard anything about Gerald, but he left his contact information and the woman on the other line promised to notify him if anything came to their attention.

He was about to go find Cindy and tell her, hoping it would ease her mind a little bit, when he realized his partner was calling.

"Liam, what do you have for me?" Mark asked as he answered his phone.

"A lot, actually. I talked to the realtor who sold Amanda's home. According to him she's not moving into an apartment."

"Oh? Where does he think she's moving to?"

"Apparently she told him that she was going to be moving in with her fiancé, but that it was just going to take a couple of weeks to straighten everything out."

"Hunh. Does this fiancé have a name?"

"No, but she told the realtor that he was very, very rich."

"I didn't see any ring on her finger."

"Neither did I. I've got a feeling I know who she thinks her fiancé is."

"This woman just gets crazier and crazier seeming," Mark said.

"Well, we're in luck. I've got the warrant."

"Why didn't you say so sooner?" Mark said, jumping down off the stool he was sitting on. "Meet you at her house?"

"Actually, I'll pick you up, I'm three minutes away."

"Perfect."

Mark quickly finished his coffee, ran upstairs and, careful not to disturb Traci, retrieved his gun and badge from his nightstand. When he made it back downstairs he found that Liam was waiting for him outside.

"Hopefully we can put an end to all this right now in time for a wonderful 'happily ever after' moment," Mark said as he slid into the passenger seat. "Weddings are stressful enough without this crap."

Four other officers met them outside Amanda's house.

"There doesn't appear to be anyone home," the first one said.

Mark nodded. "Then I want someone to keep an eye out for the homeowner. If she comes near this place I want to talk to her."

The man nodded.

The rest of them entered the house and spread out. "Okay, search everything. We're looking for anything that could tie her to Geanie, Joseph, or an assassin," Mark instructed.

Two officers headed to other parts of the house while the third started opening the boxes in the living room.

"I want a look behind that door she didn't want us looking behind," Mark said.

"Right there with you," Liam affirmed.

They strode to the back of the room and yanked open the door in question. It turned out to lead to a set of stairs heading down to what had to be a basement. Liam flipped the light switch on the wall, but they couldn't see down into the basement itself.

"Police officers," Mark called down, but there was no sound. He drew his gun, just to be on the safe side, and Liam did the same.

"I've got a bad feeling about this," Liam muttered as they walked downstairs slowly.

"Don't say that. You know what happens when you say that. Now I have a bad feeling, too. I was just feeling hopefully optimistic before."

"I call them like I see them," Liam said, barely whispering now.

Mark could feel his heart pounding. Liam's bad feeling really was contagious. There had to have been a reason Amanda didn't want them down here. She had shut the door so quickly during their visit that it had been clear that she was hiding something. He just hoped they weren't walking into some sort of trap.

When they reached the bottom, Liam reached for and flipped another light switch. Overhead lights came on revealing what looked like a guest room. Mark looked around slowly, trying to take everything in. There was no one there so he lowered his gun and next to him Liam did the same.

Mark walked further into the room. There was a bed, an overstuffed chair sitting in the corner facing the bed, and even a little kitchen table with two chairs at it. There were framed pictures hanging on the wall and everything looked almost normal.

Almost.

Mark felt his heart begin to race as a sick feeling twisted his insides. He had known that Amanda was obsessed with Joseph, but the true extent of that obsession was suddenly, horrifically clear.

"What is this place?" Liam breathed. His voice heavy with the same fear and revulsion that were vying for mastery of Mark.

Every piece of furniture had thick, heavy straps and steel shackles attached to it.

16

Mark stood in the room, struggling to take it all in. Finally he walked slowly over to one of the walls and examined the pictures hanging on it. There was a picture of Amanda wearing a wedding gown and smiling. He didn't believe he was imagining the hint of madness in her eyes. He moved on to the next photo. It was one of Joseph, clearly a publicity photo, with him wearing a dark suit and a tie. The next photo was another one of Joseph, this time a candid photo. He was half-turned away from the camera talking to someone out of sight. The final photo was of Joseph and Amanda together. Well, not exactly together. It looked like a badly photoshopped picture.

She told the realtor she'd be moving into her fiancé's house. A cold sweat broke out over his body as he looked again at the picture of her in the wedding dress. There was no doubt in his mind now that he was looking into the eyes of obsession and madness.

"What is this all for?" Liam asked.

"Not what. Who?" Mark turned toward his partner. "There's a reason Jeremiah and Joseph were stabbed with non-lethal doses of that poison. Amanda was planning on having Joseph kidnapped, and holding him down here. In her sick mind she believed she could make him love her and she would be the one he married."

"How very *Misery*," Liam said. "And with Geanie out of the way, she believed nothing would stop Joseph from loving her."

"Come on," Mark said, leading the way up the stairs. He exited outside and approached the officer there. "Any sign of her?"

"No."

"Alright I need to get pictures taken down in the basement and then I need to clear the cars out of here. I'm hoping she's coming back to the house and I don't want to spook her and miss our chance to catch her."

"Understood."

He turned to Liam. "Get out an APB on her. If she's already running or hiding we need to get on it."

Liam pulled out his phone and took a couple of steps away.

"This woman is extremely unstable," Mark told the other officer. "I have no idea if she's armed, but she should be treated as though she were incredibly dangerous."

Fifteen minutes later Mark and Liam were in the car heading back to the police station. "You know what I don't like about this?" Mark asked.

"What?"

"The poison. I don't see someone like her being able to get her hands on it."

"There was that huge cash withdrawal and the explosion at the bridal shop. It's likely she did hire someone to kidnap Joseph and kill Geanie."

"Yeah, that's the only thing that makes sense. Now, though, we have two people running around who are willing to do heaven knows what next. I have the distinct feeling that we just went from the frying pan to the fire."

"At least now we have a handle on what's going on and who is behind it. We can check out friends, family members, see if anyone's seen her in the last twelve hours or so," Liam said.

"You're talking sense, but I'm not sure how much logical behavior we can expect from her," Mark said. "That's what scares me. Sane people are predictable. Crazy people aren't."

Liam took a deep breath. "I think we can count on one thing, though."

"What's that?"

"If she's that crazy, there's no way she's just walking away, heading out of town and disappearing."

"Why's that?"

"She won't leave without Joseph."

Mark swore under his breath. "I think you're right."

Liam opened his mouth then closed it again.

"What is it?" Mark asked.

"I had an idea, but it's crazy and dangerous. You won't like it."

"We might just have to fight crazy with crazy. What do you have?"

"We can try putting a tracker on Joseph and then create a situation in which he could be easily kidnapped."

"You're right, I hate that idea. There's too many variables in play."

"That's why I didn't say anything."

Mark turned and stared out the window. He sighed. "You might be right, though. At the end of the day that might be our only play. Let's just hope it doesn't come to that."

And for the second time in a week he really wished he believed in prayer.

They made it into the office a few minutes later and Mark made a beeline for his desk. There was a report on it and he sat down to check it out.

"What is it?" Liam asked when he walked over a couple minutes later.

"They couldn't find any trace evidence on the rose. And there was no poison or anything like that on the thorns."

"Why is that making you frown?"

"Because that makes no sense. A lot of this doesn't. Who was the rose intended to be found by? Geanie? Then you would think the assassin would have poisoned it. Joseph? Then why didn't they dose it with something to knock him out?"

"Too remote for Joseph? Even if it did knock him out it would be hours after the assassin had slipped back out of the house. Unless they planned to snatch him on the way to the hospital or once there..." Liam drifted off.

"He or she could have posed as a paramedic, snatched him right there at the house with no one the wiser."

~

Six hours later there was still no sign of Amanda. Mark was beginning to worry that he and Liam had spooked her with their earlier visit. He had tried calling her only known relative, a cousin in Arizona, but the man hadn't heard from her in months. He was starting to get desperate.

"I think it's time we switch tactics," he finally told Liam.

"What do you have in mind?" his partner asked.

"I think we're going to need Joseph's help on this one."

"Want me to go get him?"

"You'd better."

Half an hour later Liam was back with Joseph and Cindy, which shouldn't have surprised Mark and yet it did. The four of them set up with a tech guy in one of the interrogation rooms. They were getting ready to track Amanda's phone once she picked up after Joseph called. *If* she picked up. She hadn't answered when Mark had tried the phone earlier. She was so obsessed with Joseph, though, that Mark was willing to bet she'd managed to get his phone number and that when she saw it was him calling she wouldn't be able to resist answering.

"Are you sure you're okay to do this?" Mark asked.

"Do we really have any other choice?" Joseph said.

"No," Mark admitted.

"Then, I'm okay to do this," Joseph said.

"That was circular," Liam noted.

Mark glared at him and his partner just shook his head.

Joseph dialed and Mark held his breath, hoping that Amanda would pick up. One ring. Two. Three.

"Hello?"

"Hi, Amanda? This is Joseph Coulter."

"Joseph?" she said, sounding slightly dazed.

"How are you?" he asked.

"I'm fine, why are you calling?" she asked, suspicion creeping into her voice.

Mark cringed. They needed to keep her on the phone a lot longer and the last thing they needed was her realizing for sure that they were onto her.

"Actually, I'm calling because I never got your RSVP to the wedding. You're one of just a few I haven't heard back from so I'm calling to find out whether or not you'll be making it. I need to give the final headcount to the caterer this afternoon."

"Your wedding? You invited me to your wedding?" she asked, a little breathless now.

"Of course. You got the invitation, right?" Joseph said, sounding impressively concerned.

"No."

"Oh no, really? Hold on, I've got the master address list here somewhere. Yes. I sent your invitation to 1418 Larkspur Drive. You should have received it about four weeks ago."

"I live at 1413 Larkspur Drive," she said, clearly distressed.

"Really? Oh, I'm terribly sorry. I must have misread the 3 as an 8 when I was making the list."

"Th-that's okay."

"Well, the wedding is this Saturday at 4 o'clock. I'm sorry that you never received the invitation and it's such short notice, but do you think you can make it?"

"I'll be there," she said.

"I'm so glad to hear that. Do you have a pen and a piece of paper so I can give you the address?" Joseph asked, oozing sincerity.

"I know where it's going to be."

"Oh, you do?"

"I saw the announcement in the newspaper."

"Oh, I see. Well, I'm officially putting you in the attending column. Will you be bringing a guest?"

"A guest?"

"Yes, the invitation, which you sadly didn't get, said that you could bring a guest if you liked."

"Oh, um, no guest. Just me."

"Okay."

Mark gave Joseph the thumbs up sign. Off to the side Liam was already directing officers to her location.

"Alright, well, I guess I'll be seeing you on Saturday."

"Yes, thank you," she breathed.

Joseph ended the call and then collapsed back in his chair.

"You did great," Mark reassured him.

"That was one of the hardest things I've ever had to do," Joseph admitted. "I don't think I'm cut out to be an actor."

"Well, you could have fooled me. You were great, really."

Cindy squeezed Joseph's hand and he gave her a weak smile.

"Now what?" Joseph asked.

"Now, we wait, and hope for good news."

Fifteen minutes later Liam's phone rang. He listened intently for a few minutes before hanging up. "She was at a Starbuck's across from Stoneridge Mall. When they got there she was gone. They searched the nearby area but found no sign of her. They did, however, find her phone under a table. They couldn't tell if she dropped it on purpose or by accident. She didn't talk to anyone inside other than to order a coffee," he reported.

Mark closed his eyes and tried to swallow his frustration. "Back to square one," he said at last. He opened his eyes and looked at Joseph. "I'm sorry."

Joseph shook his head. "Not at all. It was worth a try."

Cindy leaned forward suddenly. "You said she was at the Starbuck's across from Stoneridge Mall?"

"Yes, why?"

"There's a formalwear shop in that mall on the second floor. What if she hung up with Joseph and immediately went to buy herself a dress?"

"It's a long shot, but if you're right, she could still be in there," Mark said.

"I'm on it," Liam said, whipping out his phone.

Once he was off the phone Mark stood. "Okay, hopefully they find something. For now I've got to get you two back to the mansion."

~

By the time they were pulling up in front of the mansion Liam had called Mark with the bad news. Amanda had been in the dress store. She'd stayed less than ten minutes, bought a dress, and had been gone before police arrived.

"Well, at least your instincts were right on," Mark said with a sigh.

"Unfortunately, that's little comfort at the moment," Cindy said, feeling the frustration building inside her.

"And it's a safe bet she's going to show to the wedding."

"Isn't that what every guy wants? His bride and his stalker both in the same place?" Joseph said, forcing a smile.

Cindy was relieved to see that the others had already started setting up for the afternoon barbeque. She'd been able to call everyone that morning who wasn't staying at the mansion to let them know the barbeque was off. At Geanie's insistence she didn't explain about the danger that the couple was in but simply said that Geanie had been injured during the downtown explosion a few days before and was still recovering. It was a bit more than stretching the truth, but Geanie was determined that no one outside those who needed to know be made aware that they had been attacked. She had argued that would just bring publicity that would make everyone's jobs harder and bring stress and anxiety to their guests which could mar the occasion. Everyone had been gracious, passing along wishes for Geanie to rest up before the wedding.

Dave greeted the car as it pulled up. He was carrying a couple of packages of Caspar hot dogs out toward the barbeque area.

"You're just in time," he said cheerfully. "We decided to get this party started sooner rather than later."

"Sounds like a plan," Cindy said.

"Got to warn you, though. In my family I've won the Annual Fourth of July Croquet Match of Ultimate Glory four years in a row."

Cindy found herself shaking her head. "You must have a really interesting family."

"Are you kidding? My parents are both crazier than I am," he said with a grin.

Mark shook his head as he got out of the car. "I want to check on Traci and then I should get back to the station."

He headed into the house while Cindy followed Dave out to the barbeque pit adjacent to where the croquet lawn had already been set up. Jeremiah was busy studying one of the mallets.

"Checking for perfect weight and balance?" she teased.

"Thinking that it would make a good weapon," he said absently.

"How hard would you have to swing one of these to kill someone?"

"Not as hard as you would think." He turned suddenly toward her, looking slightly flustered. "If it came to that," he added.

"Well, let's hope we can keep this a friendly game," she said with a smile.

"I think that would be best for all concerned, yes," he said, smiling back.

"Did I miss anything?"

"No. How did things go for you guys?"

"Joseph managed to get her on the phone. They pinpointed her location but missed her."

"Shame."

"You don't sound surprised."

"I'm not. When are our lives ever that easy?"

She sighed. "A girl can hope, can't she?"

"We're about to have company," he said.

She turned and looked back at the house. People were beginning to pour out of it and they each seemed to be carrying some kind of bowl or platter. "That's going to be a lot of food."

"Dorothy and Charlotte were in the kitchen for a couple of hours. I think it's safe to say that no one's going to go hungry this afternoon," he said.

There was a long table set up near the grill and people began to pile the food on there. Finished, they turned right back around.

"More food?" Cindy marveled.

She had guessed wrong. A minute later everyone trooped out carrying folding chairs.

"I really should go help," she said.

"It's okay. They all need to feel like they're doing something, being helpful. You're more than doing your part."

"Doesn't feel like it. It's weird. There's nothing to look up, nothing to research. We know who the bad guys are. There's just nothing I can do to help find them."

"It's okay," he said, putting a hand on her shoulder.

"No, it's not. I feel useless, like all I can do is sit and wait on other people for stuff. I'm waiting for the Pine Springs police to catch the killers. I'm waiting for the New Orleans police to figure out what happened to Gerald. I'm waiting for Gerald to figure out what he was going to tell me about Matthew and Paul."

"Most of human life is spent waiting," Jeremiah said. "Waiting at the store, for the weekend, waiting for that next big life event, waiting for the holidays, or waiting for that perfect person."

"Or waiting for that perfect moment," she muttered.

"Yes," he said softly.

She watched as Joseph approached the barbeque with a look of joy on his face. The others were gathering around the food table, laughing and chatting. They were living in the moment, enjoying it as best they could despite everything that had been happening, still might happen.

While she was just...waiting.

She looked up at Jeremiah and he looked down at her with an expression she couldn't read. Sometimes she could tell exactly what he was thinking. Other times it was as though he was wearing a mask and she couldn't even get the slightest hint of his emotions, his thoughts. She hated that. It was like there were times when he was shutting her out, though there were less and less of those moments the longer they knew each other. Sometimes she felt like she knew him so well and other times she worried that she didn't know him at all.

Something had happened to him in his past. That much she was certain of. One of these days she hoped he might actually share with her what it was. Until then, though, there was the mask. Maybe one day he'd finally take it off.

"Uh oh, something's wrong," Jeremiah said.

She turned and followed his line of sight.

Mark was heading toward them at a jog and even she could tell that he wasn't happy about something.

She braced herself for whatever bad news he was about to deliver. She expected him to head over to Joseph but instead he came straight to them.

"What is it, what's happened?" Cindy asked, heart in her throat.

"I just talked to an officer from the New Orleans Police Department."

Her chest constricted. Gerald. The call had to have been about him. She felt Jeremiah squeeze her shoulder and she reached up and grabbed his hand.

"What's happened to Gerald?" she asked.

"He was admitted to a hospital there early this morning with stab wounds to both the throat and abdomen."

"Oh no!"

"Apparently they've got their best doctors working on him, but it's touch and go right now. They've got a police guard on him, and they'll let us know the moment anything changes."

"Did he say anything?" Jeremiah asked.

"No, he was found and brought in unconscious." Mark hesitated and then reached out and touched Cindy's arm. "He's not expected to make it."

17

Jeremiah felt terrible for Cindy, even worse than he felt for Geanie and Joseph. Geanie and Joseph had each other to cling to. To make things even worse, Cindy felt responsible for what had happened to Gerald. He wished there was some way he could comfort her, but just like her, just like everyone else in the mansion, he was stuck waiting.

"It's like some old Agatha Christie novel," Veronica commented Tuesday evening.

"If it was, one of us would be the killer," Traci said.

They were all in the dining room playing board games. They had made it through the rest of Sunday and all of Monday without any incidents. Instead of making everyone relax, though, it seemed to just be building the sense of anticipation. It reminded Jeremiah of the paranoia that could sometimes settle over those with dangerous jobs as they were nearing retirement. There was a sense that there might not be any getting out of this alive and so the more time passed, the greater the odds something was going to happen.

Lyle, the final member of the wedding party, was scheduled to arrive that evening, and at least that would be a welcome distraction. Joseph had called him a couple of days before and explained the situation, telling him he was free to back out with no hard feelings. Lyle had insisted on coming anyway. Given Jeremiah's mood he vacillated between thinking Lyle was loyal and Lyle was stupid.

"The only killer here is Jeremiah," Joseph said.

Jeremiah looked up sharply.

"No matter what game we play he slaughters the rest of us."

Jeremiah mentally chided himself. He shouldn't be playing so competitively. It was not smart.

"You say that, but watch, I'm sure I'll lose now for the rest of the night," he said with a smile.

"You honestly think your winning streak is over?" Jordan asked. Jordan was the ministry leader for the singles ministry at First Shepherd. Apparently he and Joseph had been friends since they were kids. "Just like that?" Jordan said with a snap.

Jeremiah shrugged.

He knew it was over. He would be throwing every game the rest of the night, but subtly so no one would realize that's what he was doing.

It had been difficult, living with people for so many days. He lived alone and at home he could relax, let his guard down, and be himself. Here, though, he had to be constantly on alert. He couldn't even relax when he was alone in his room. And with no ability to retreat, to go somewhere else, *anywhere* else for even just an hour or two it was getting really difficult.

What made it even harder was the fact that some of these people knew him fairly well. At least, they thought they did, and he was used to being slightly more relaxed around them. The same was not true for everyone, though, so he found himself caught between levels of familiarity.

There was a face he showed to the world. Then there was the face he reserved for people who were more like friends like Geanie and Joseph. Then there was the face that he had shown Mark, allowing the detective to see more than most. Finally there was the face that he let Cindy see. It was the best of him, and, occasionally, also parts of the worst of him. But only parts.

He knew he was confusing Cindy, Geanie, and Joseph because he had the walls firmly up. He couldn't help it, though. There were too many strangers and casual acquaintances around. They hadn't earned his trust, nor the right to see anything but the carefully cultivated persona he had crafted for himself when he came to Pine Springs.

He knew that while other people would say that they had friends they could let their hair down and be themselves around, that their social role-playing was as nothing compared to his. Regular people were who they were. They might be more uninhibited at some times than others, but usually what you saw was what you got. His outer image and his inner self hadn't matched in a long, long time.

"Jeremiah, it's your turn," Traci prodded.

"Sorry," he said, studying the game board.

Around him people were laughing, trying to make the best of a bad situation. The forced intimacy of all of them having to be together all the time had broken down barriers for the rest of them. Teasing and fake insults were flying around the table.

"I'm still sorry we couldn't all go to The Zone yesterday," Joseph said.

"It's not your fault," Traci said.

"I know, but I still wanted to see Wildman barf after going on The Atomic Coaster."

"Oh no, there's no way I'll ever go on that thing again," Dave said, rolling his eyes.

"How many kids was it that you threw up on during that one church trip?" Cindy asked.

"None," Dave said, trying his best to have a poker face.

"I heard it was ten," Geanie said.

"It was only four," Dave said, turning red in the face.

"Only four?" Dorothy said with a laugh.

"You threw up on four kids at the same time?" Veronica asked.

"It was epic," Jordan said. "I was there. I'll never forget it as long as I live."

Jeremiah played his turn and sat back. He did have to admit that the thought of Dave throwing up on the kids was hilarious. Usually it was kids who managed to throw up on adults. "I would have paid to see that," he said, forcing a smile.

Smile, joke. That's what a normal person would do. Why was it the longer he was stuck in this cage the harder it was to act normal?

"I need to get some fresh air," Mark said at the conclusion of the game. "I'll be back in a couple."

"I think I'll go with you," Jeremiah said, hastily getting to his feet.

"Alright, fifteen minute break to take care of...whatever," Dave said. "Be back here then. We're teaming up for Trivial Pursuit."

Once outside they walked away from the house, past the first officer on guard.

"Is it just me or is the tension ratcheted up so high I think there's going to be some kind of explosion?" Mark asked.

"It's not just you."

"Oh good. I thought I was going crazy by myself. Nice to see I have company."

"I think all of us could probably use some downtime. Certainly some alone time."

"I hear you, but I can't make that happen."

Jeremiah refrained from pointing out that Mark could, in fact, make it happen, he just didn't want to.

"So, what do you know about this Lyle guy who should be here soon?" Mark asked.

"Not much. He and Joseph were friends in college. I know they hang out every time they're in the same city."

"Friendship," Mark grunted. "It's a weird thing. See, by that description I would never guess Lyle would be willing to risk his neck to be here during all this madness."

"I know."

"You never can tell, though. Sometimes you think you have a best friend and they turn their back on you when you need them. Other times the person you just thought of as a casual friend goes through hell for you without you even asking."

"Who are we talking about now?" Jeremiah asked.

Mark threw back his head and stared up at the moon. "You know, I never had a lot of friends. Not naturally the trusting type I guess."

"It comes with the badge I'd guess."

"I was this way even as a kid. Then again, even when I was a kid I knew I wanted to be a cop when I grew up. I was always interrogating everyone I could get my hands on. If there was a mystery to solve I was right in the middle of it."

"Must have been fun for your parents."

Mark shook his head. "What I'm trying to say is that two years ago if someone had told me my best friends were going to be a rabbi and a church secretary, I would have laughed in their face."

"Because we're religious or we're not cops?"

"Because I never thought I'd really have best friends."

Jeremiah didn't know what to say.

"You know what the craziest part about it is?" Mark asked.

"What?"

"You're my best friends and yet the thought of hanging out with you socially makes me twitch."

Jeremiah chuckled. "Whenever you do spend time with us it's always been because bad things are happening, and if not they will shortly. Subconsciously you equate seeing us with-"

"Death and destruction?" Mark interrupted.

"Something like that," Jeremiah said.

"Well, that makes sense I guess. So, the solution would be, what? Squeeze in friend time with everything else."

"I don't have the answers."

"Maybe. Maybe not. I do have one question, though."

Jeremiah tensed. "What is it?" The contents of the note Mark had received flashed through his mind. *Ask him what his name is.*

"Why are you religious?"

"What?" Jeremiah asked, taken completely off guard.

"A man finds out he's going to be a father, he starts to ask himself the big questions."

"Ah, like 'Is there a G-d'?"

"Exactly. So, I want to know why you believe what you do."

"I was raised in a religious home. My family believed very strongly. It made sense to me, it helped explain so much of the world around me, especially given all the uncertainty and strife. I always believed and I studied the Torah as much as I could."

"Just like I knew I wanted to be a cop you knew you wanted to be a rabbi."

Jeremiah smiled. "Perhaps, but, being a rabbi did not enter my mind when I was young. I was thirsty for knowledge, of G-d and his creation. Then, when I grew up, and joined the army for my requisite service, I found I needed G-d more than ever."

Mark nodded. "My parents didn't believe in anything they couldn't see or touch. Religion was right out for them. My dad always drilled into me that everything is logical; that everything has a rational explanation."

"And you believed him."

"I did for a long time."

"What changed that?" Jeremiah asked.

"One day I was called out to a murder scene. Sixteen-year-old boy had been killed, run over. I thought it was a hit-and-run or possibly something gang related. Then I caught the kid who did it. He ran him over on purpose, but he didn't even know him. I asked him why he did it. I mean, all the murders I worked there was always a reason, money, jealousy, something. This kid just laughed and said he did it because he could. That was the day I stopped believing that everything had a logical explanation, that the world made sense."

"I can see why. Pure evil for evil's sake is a hard thing for most people to grasp."

"Yeah, well, what can you do?" Mark said.

Jeremiah could tell that the conversation was over. He didn't know if Mark had been satisfied with the answer he'd given him, but it was the only one he had.

Mark's phone rang and he answered it. "You got him? Good. Okay. Thanks."

"An officer is driving Lyle here. So, shall we get back inside and see who's going to clean the floor with who during Trivial Pursuit?"

"You've got it," Jeremiah said with a smile.

~

Cindy was relieved when Thursday rolled around. It felt like they were finally in the home stretch and soon everything would be over. It also meant she and the other bridesmaids got to decorate the formal living room and dining room for the bachelorette party while Geanie spent some time with her parents.

The only other person Cindy had originally invited to the bachelorette party was Sylvia from work who fortunately already understood the nature of what they were all going through. It was agreed that just to be on the safe side she wouldn't come. However, Mark was nice enough to swing by the church and pick up the present she had been planning on bringing.

When it was finally time Cindy went and got Geanie. She led the other woman over to the other wing of the house and then slowly pushed open the door to the formal living room.

"Welcome," Cindy said, "to the point of no return."

Geanie squealed with delight and clapped her hands.

Phantom of the Opera music was playing and Cindy and the others had decorated the room with white and black streamers and balloons. Red roses were scattered throughout the area. They'd even managed to scare up a fog machine so that they had to walk through the fog into the room just as if they were descending into the Phantom's lair.

"You guys are just the best," Geanie said when they were seated in the formal living room.

"Oh sure, you say that now, but let's see what you're saying when the night's over," Traci said with a laugh.

"I'm sure I'll love you all even more!"

"Ooh, she's a brave one," Veronica said.

"You know what they say, marriage is not for the faint of heart," Traci deadpanned.

The evening went beautifully. The games were fun and there was tons of screaming and teasing. It turned out everyone had bought Geanie lingerie. Quite by coincidence she actually opened the presents in order from least raciest to most. Traci's gift was last and was tiny and completely see-through.

"I couldn't possibly wear this," Geanie said, blushing.

"Give it two weeks," Traci said with a laugh.

~

Mark was nearing the end of the line. He was beyond exhausted and running out of ideas. He had to do a lot of last minute rearranging and with difficulty he managed to beg off the bachelor party. He planned to spend the time working out more details for the next two days but instead he fell asleep.

When he woke in the morning he at least felt a bit better. He was the only one who didn't yawn all the way through breakfast.

"Given that I know there was no liquor at either party, I must say you people know how to party like madmen," he finally commented.

"Arrive first, leave last," Geanie said.

"What did I miss?" he teased.

"Pool championship," Jeremiah said.

"Epic pillow fight," Cindy answered.

"Okay, the girls definitely had the better party," he said with a grin.

~

Evening had rolled around and they were all dressed nicely for the rehearsal and the dinner. Everyone was standing in the entryway while Mark presided in front of the doors like a general.

"So, here's the plan. We have the limo we'll be using tomorrow. It's going to stay with us, and tonight we'll use it as well. The driver is one of our officers," Mark said.

"They really aren't taking any chances," Jeremiah whispered to Cindy.

They all walked outside and piled into the car. Cindy found herself squished up next to Jeremiah and she felt herself flush.

"It's going to be a bit tight in here. We had originally planned for two cars and no police escort," Joseph said apologetically.

"We can all squeeze," Geanie said. "It will be good practice for tomorrow when my dress will need lots of room."

Everyone laughed and squished together more. Jeremiah put his arm on the back of the seat behind Cindy to give her more room and the feel of his arm against her shoulders just made her blush harder.

The ceremony was going to be happening at First Shepherd. The reception was at a huge banquet hall ten minutes away. They were supposed to have spent the morning decorating the banquet hall with all the favors and everything else. Officers had been sweeping the hall all day, though, looking for anything suspicious. They weren't going to be able to get in there until the morning when it was going to be all hands on deck to get everything done on time.

The ride to the church was over too quickly for Cindy. They all piled into the church and were met by the minister who was officiating.

For a miracle the rehearsal went smoothly. When it was over they were driven to Rue de Main where Joseph had proposed to Geanie. The French restaurant was beautiful, and it had been booked out just for them.

Cindy sat next to Geanie while Jeremiah sat on the other side of Joseph at a round table that could seat six. Geanie's parents took the other two places.

The food was amazing and the atmosphere completely romantic. The restaurant had Phantom of the Opera music playing softly in the background.

Despite the elegance of the setting Cindy struggled with an almost overwhelming desire to throw a bit of her bread at Jeremiah. She didn't know why, maybe just to get his attention, maybe just to do something to cut the tension that was still building.

She looked around the room and she could tell everyone else was feeling it. Behind the laughter and the smiles there were eyes with dark circles under them and strained looks whenever the laughter ceased for even a moment. Another twenty-four hours and it would all be over, one way or another. She just prayed that everyone would be safe and nothing would ruin the wedding.

Dinner progressed, and she felt herself slowly starting to relax. It was good to be away from the mansion. It was lovely, but a week stuck inside with all the pressure they were under was beginning to cause its own issues.

Cindy glanced up from her meal and froze. There, staring in through the restaurant window was the same man who had been staring into the bridal shop window hours before it blew up.

18

"That's him!" Cindy shrieked, lunging out of her chair and pointing out the window. "I saw him outside the bridal shop watching us the day it blew up!"

Jeremiah leaped to his feet, catching a glimpse of the man's face before it disappeared. He raced toward the entrance and a moment later he was out on the street, twisting his head right and left and searching for the man. He finally spotted him ducking down a side street.

Jeremiah chased after him, aware that there was someone following him as well. He hoped it was Mark, but he didn't have time to stop and look. He turned the corner just in time to see the man turn another corner.

Jeremiah put on a fresh burst of speed. He neared the corner, heard the sound of a car engine, rounded the corner and then jumped back as a black car thundered by. It nearly ran him over and he turned, fuming when he saw that the license plates had been removed from the car.

He turned and came face-to-face with Mark. "Did you get the plate number?" Mark asked.

Jeremiah shook his head. "He had removed the plates."

For a moment he thought Mark was going to punch the brick wall next to them. Finally he pulled himself together.

"Let's go get the others and get out of here before the restaurant blows up or something."

"They're boxing up our desserts to go," Cindy announced when the two men walked back in.

"You must be some kind of mind reader," Mark grumbled.

"No, that would be me, actually," Traci said with a strained smile.

"Cindy, you're sure it was the same man you saw outside the bridal shop?" Mark asked.

"Yes, I hadn't even remembered him until I saw him peeking in here, just the same way. I couldn't get a good look at him either time because he had his hand up to his eyes, but I'd swear it was the same guy."

"I didn't get a good enough look at him to identify him either," Jeremiah said.

Mark just shook his head, muttering something under his breath.

~

Five minutes later they were in the limo heading back to the house. Once there Milt and Dorothy called it a night and the others took their desserts and adjourned to the living room.

Mark was anxious and he could tell the others were feeling it, too. "Okay, we need to talk about tomorrow and about the logistics."

"One of your officers will be driving the limo tomorrow to the church. We're leaving here at two which will give everyone plenty of time to get ready at the church," Joseph said.

"I had officers sweep it earlier today looking for anything unusual. A couple will be posted there all night to make sure that nothing is tampered with," Mark said. "And tomorrow, all of Pine Springs PD will be there and then some."

"Wow, that sounds like overkill," Joseph said.

"More like 'avoid a kill'," Mark noted grimly. "Tomorrow the watchword is security, security, security. No one goes anywhere alone, not even the bathroom, is that understood?"

All around him heads bobbed up and down.

"Now, we're going to be securing the banquet hall as well, but my gut tells me they're going to strike at the wedding, before the minister pronounces Joseph and Geanie husband and wife."

"That would seem in keeping with Amanda's goals," Cindy said.

"We need to get in that banquet hall for decorating it in the morning," Geanie reminded.

"Eight a.m. someone will take you there and then bring you back at noon. Remember, if you see anyone or anything suspicious, you report in."

"Any chance the security will scare them off?" Dave asked.

"I don't think so," Mark said, shaking his head. "Besides, at Geanie and Joseph's request, most of the officers will be dressed as wedding guests."

Geanie grimaced. "It's bad enough we all have to be stressed out, I didn't want to have to explain to the whole world what was going on. If all goes well they'll catch these people and only we'll be the wiser and everyone can go about the business of enjoying the day."

"I know this would be awful, but has anyone considered postponing the wedding?" Lyle asked.

"It might calm things down, for now, but even if it did, I have a feeling we'd just be right back here in three months or whatever it was," Mark said.

"And frankly, Geanie and I won't wait any longer," Joseph said. "We'll elope if we have to," he said, threading his fingers through hers. "It's not our first choice, but we have been talking about if it would be better, safer for everyone. For all of you. I mean, we appreciate everything you guys have done, everything you've risked, but we want to protect you."

"But, that's not how it's supposed to be," Veronica said.

"Excuse me?" Mark asked.

"You guys aren't supposed to be protecting us, we're supposed to be protecting you."

"Actually that's the job of the police," Mark said.

"No, you don't understand what I mean," Veronica said.

"Okay, then what exactly do you mean?" he asked.

"You know what the original reason, the original purpose for having bridesmaids and groomsmen was?" Veronica asked.

"No, What was it?" Mark asked, surprised that she was speaking up and a little irritated because he didn't see how something like that could be relevant to the discussion at hand.

"The attendants dressed in festive clothes similar to the bride and groom to confuse evil spirits and keep them from attacking the couple."

Before he could say anything Traci reached out and grabbed Veronica's hand, "That's brilliant," she said.

"Do you think it will work?" Charlotte asked.

"It has to, and given one of Geanie's surprises for the wedding, I think it just might," Cindy said, her voice shaking with excitement.

"It's too dangerous, I won't stand for it," Geanie said, face pale.

Mark blinked at them. "Would one of you ladies care to tell me what's going on in that group mind you're apparently sharing?"

They all turned and stared at him as if he was a complete moron.

"Amanda and her hired killer may be flesh and blood instead of spirit, but they're still evil," Veronica said.

"And if we play this right, they should be just as easy to confuse," Cindy said.

"I still have no idea what you're talking about," Mark said.

"I think I'm catching on to the idea, but I'm baffled as to how you ladies think you can execute it," Jeremiah said.

"Because us ladies know something you gentlemen don't," Charlotte said.

"I think it's time we showed them," Cindy said, standing up. "Geanie?"

Geanie took a deep breath and then nodded. "Yes, yes, it's time they knew what we've been planning."

"I'm going to hate this, aren't I?" Mark asked.

Joseph stood hesitantly and grabbed Geanie's hand, his eyes troubled. "You worked so long and hard to keep this a surprise. Are you sure you want to reveal it now?"

Geanie stared intently into Joseph's eyes. "Dear, husband-to-be, I love you more than anything. And I think God was leading both of us to this moment, to these decisions that just might help save our lives even as we are pledging them to each other. You know I don't believe in accidents, coincidences. I think I was meant to do what I did. I think I'm also meant to reveal it now. Trust me."

And then she smiled at him with such love that it even moved Mark who cleared his throat and looked away. He found Traci's eyes and she stared at him with the same love only magnified by all they had seen and experienced together. He smiled and reached out for her hand.

"Come and see," she said softly. "All will be made clear."

Together they all headed to the study that the women had declared off limits days ago. With great ceremony Geanie opened the door and led the way inside. At the far end of the room were tables with dozens of boxes. Geanie led the way over to one of them and opened the top.

She pulled out a carnival mask, like one might see in Venice. She turned and smiled. "These are for the reception. They are the favors that each guest can take home." She turned it over and there, printed on the inside of the mask, were her and Joseph's names and the date.

"The reception will be a sort of impromptu masquerade, in honor of Joseph's proposing to me with songs from Phantom of the Opera, beginning with "Masquerade".

She replaced it in the box and then moved to the end of the table to a much smaller box. She opened the lid slowly, reverently, then drew two objects out. In her one hand she held a mask clearly inspired by the Phantom of the Opera one. In the other she held a beautiful white silk mask covered with feathers and pearls. "These are for Joseph and I. There are gold ones for the rest of the bridal party. It was my intention that we enter the reception wearing them, but what the ladies are suggesting is that we all don our masks a little sooner, at the wedding. I confess, I had been strongly considering that already. The difference, here, is that they are also suggesting that Joseph and I disguise ourselves as attendants and that two of them take our places until the assassin can be discovered."

Mark gaped slowly, looking around the room at all the sincere faces staring back at him. "You're insane, all of you," he said at last.

"In order for this to work," Traci said, "no one but the eleven of us must know of the charade."

"Agreed," the others echoed.

"You're out of your minds!" Mark said. "How could you even consider this? Whoever stands up there as bride and groom are risking their lives, regardless of who they are. You can't think this is a good idea."

"It's the only way," Dave said softly.

"Even if I thought you were right, who would assume such an enormous risk?"

"I will stand in for Geanie," Cindy said.

"And I will stand in for Joseph," Jeremiah said.

The two of them looked at each other and a silent understanding seemed to pass between them.

Mark stared at them. "Now, yes, now is the time."

"The time for what?" Cindy asked.

"I think now would be a good time to pray," he whispered.

~

It was a crazy idea. So crazy, it just might work, Jeremiah reflected as he watched the sanctuary filling up with people the next afternoon. He and Joseph were waiting in the wings, masks already firmly in place. Mark was waiting with them.

"This is insanity," Mark hissed.

"But inspired insanity, you have to admit," Joseph said. Mark sighed.

Jeremiah just kept a watchful eye out, wondering when one of their uninvited guests was finally going to show. He'd barely slept at all the night before, thinking about what this day was going to entail. Trying not to think about what Cindy was going to look like wearing that wedding dress and walking down the aisle toward him. Every time the thought crossed his mind he lost all ability to concentrate on anything else.

If he was feeling this way he could only imagine how Joseph was feeling.

"Five minutes 'til," Mark told them. "Those ladies had better start this show on time. I can't stand the suspense much longer."

"Imagine how we're feeling," Joseph said, nudging Jeremiah in the ribs. Jeremiah forced himself to smile even though the implication that he should be as nervous as Joseph struck a nerve. The truth was he figured he was more nervous than Joseph. And not for the reasons Mark would guess.

They had been able to decorate the banquet hall that morning, all of them working together. It was going to look amazing. If anyone made it that far.

~

"You look beautiful," Geanie said to Cindy.

Cindy turned, her hands shaking as she smoothed down the white dress that her friend should have been wearing instead of her. "Thank you. And you look amazing."

It was true. Wearing Cindy's fuchsia maid of honor gown Geanie had never looked so radiant. She looked around at the rest of the room. Veronica, Charlotte, and Traci were wearing their forest green gowns and also looked beautiful. All of them were wearing their hair up in matching hairstyles. Each of them had a gold mask in one hand and a bouquet of roses in the other.

What had seemed so clear and like such a good idea the night before was now making her stomach churn with anxiety that had nothing to do with the killer who was on the loose.

Even though it was all a masquerade, she was the one who was going to be walking down the aisle, and she was going to be walking toward Jeremiah. She got lightheaded every time she thought about it.

"Are you ready?" Geanie asked Cindy.

"I think that's my line," Cindy said, hating that she could hear her own voice shaking.

Geanie smiled and slipped her mask on. The other women did the same. It was actually nearly impossible to tell them apart, she realized with a start. Cindy took a deep breath and then donned the white mask.

"Let's get this show on the road," she said.

Geanie pushed open the door to the small room the women had used to change in. One by one Charlotte, Veronica, and Traci filed out. Then Geanie followed, and after a moment's hesitation Cindy went after her. They walked slowly to the closed doors at the back of the sanctuary.

The place was packed. So many people were attending the wedding that they'd had to put overflow seating in the gymnasium and set up a large screen television in there. Police officers dressed as wedding guests were positioned all over, searching for Amanda or the assassin she had hired. Cindy couldn't help but wonder if there had been this much security at the real Royal Wedding.

They all paused outside the closed sanctuary doors. Dave, Jordan, and Lyle were already waiting for them there.

"This is it," Geanie whispered, barely able to keep the excitement out of her voice.

The doors opened and she could hear a harp playing *All I Ask of You*. Jordan and Charlotte went down first. They were followed by Lyle and Veronica. Then Dave and Traci went down. Geanie walked down alone as Joseph was waiting up front with Jeremiah. Cindy felt a pang of sorrow for her friend that she wasn't getting to walk down the aisle to the Wedding March.

The Wedding March started and Cindy froze for a moment, nearly overcome with terror. Then she forced herself to move one foot forward then the other. Everyone rose as she entered the sanctuary. She kept glancing from side to side wondering where the killer was, wondering when disaster would strike. She kept looking everywhere, desperately avoiding looking forward.

When she finally did her heart leapt. She recognized Jeremiah, even though he was wearing the mask. It was the way he held himself and she realized she would know him anywhere. She forced herself to keep walking.

She reached the stairs and walked up them. Jeremiah stepped forward to take her hand and her skin tingled where he was touching it. She barely remembered to hand her bouquet to Traci.

"You look beautiful," Jeremiah whispered for her ears alone.

"And you so very handsome," she managed to say around the lump in her throat.

The music stopped, everyone sat, and Cindy tried to calm herself. Surely the attack must come at any moment. Amanda had fantasies of marrying Joseph herself; she'd never stand to see him marry Geanie.

"Dearly beloved, we are gathered here in the eyes of God, to join this man and this woman in holy matrimony," the minister began. That was when Cindy made the mistake of looking into Jeremiah's eyes.

The world seemed to stop and it was just the two of them, caught up in this moment together. Slowly, he reached forward and took her other hand so that he was holding both of them. Even though he was wearing a mask she felt like at that moment it was the first time she was really seeing him.

"Which is commended to be honorable among all men; and therefore is not by any to be entered into unadvisedly or lightly, but reverently, discreetly, advisedly and solemnly. Into this holy estate these two persons present now come to be joined," the minister continued.

She could feel warmth spreading throughout her body even as part of her began to panic.

"If any person can show just cause why they may not be joined together, let them speak now or forever hold their peace."

She sucked in her breath. This was it, the moment of truth, the moment when surely one of the uninvited guests would announce their presence.

Silence, and nothing more.

Then the minister was moving on. He was speaking about love, and what it was, and what it wasn't. Cindy could only half hear him because her mind was racing. It should be over now. She shouldn't still be standing here. She started to take a step back, but Jeremiah squeezed her hands harder.

She glanced past him to the wings where she could see Mark waiting. The detective nodded once at her then turned to sweep the crowd with his eyes. *He wants us to keep going*, Cindy realized, starting to get dizzy. Her knees started to give way, but before she could collapse, Jeremiah stepped forward and put his hands on her waist, holding her up. She put her hands on his upper arms. She could feel the play of his muscles beneath her fingers.

"Is everything alright?" the minister whispered low.

"Just a little dizzy," Cindy managed to whisper back.

"Don't worry, my love, I've got you," Jeremiah said, his voice husky.

The minister continued and they just stood there, Cindy holding on to Jeremiah for dear life while he held her on her feet.

"And now, the exchanging of the vows," the minister said. "First you," he said, addressing Cindy. "Repeat after me."

"I take thee as my wedded husband."

"I take thee as my wedded husband," she said.

"To have and to hold from this day forward."

"To have...and to...hold from this day forward."

"For better, for worse, for richer, for poorer, in sickness or in health."

"For better, for worse, for richer, for poorer, in sickness or in health." She just kept staring up at Jeremiah. He was smiling bigger than she'd ever seen him smile. His eyes behind the mask were sparkling. She finally risked a glance at Joseph and realized that Jeremiah looked even happier than him.

"To love and to cherish 'til death do us part."

"To love and to cherish 'til death -"

The sanctuary was plunged suddenly into darkness.

19

Jeremiah blinked for a moment in the sudden darkness. The happy haze that had been enveloping him a moment before burst like a bubble. It was happening. He had rehearsed his exit dozens of times throughout the afternoon. He knew the steps by heart even if he had to take them in the dark.

He scooped Cindy up in his arms, turned and headed for the side exit to the sanctuary where Mark was waiting. Only when he got there the detective was gone. Hopefully that meant he was chasing down one of the bad guys.

He made it out the side, turned toward the front of the sanctuary and crashed to his knees as something struck him sharply on the back of the neck. His vision swam before his eyes and it was all he could do to hold on to Cindy who was now screaming and thrashing.

He felt someone grab him under his armpits and then a moment later release him.

He heard a shout and a moment later a flashlight hit him full in the face.

"Tell me your real name," Mark demanded.

It was such an eerie echo of the thing Jeremiah had been dreading him asking that it took his breath away for a moment. "It's me, Jeremiah," he managed to whisper at last as Cindy stopped struggling. "Behind me."

Mark ran past him, as Jeremiah struggled to retain consciousness.

~

Mark made it out of the sanctuary just in time to see a black-clad figure disappear around the corner of the building. He raced forward, rounded the corner and kept running, trying to figure out where the assailant had gone next.

If it hadn't been for the tiniest flash of what looked like peach fabric disappearing inside Mark would have run right past the one darkened meeting room. The clerk at the store in the mall had said that Amanda had bought a peach dress.

He spun on his heel and moved silently toward the entrance of the room, pressing himself against the outside wall and waving several other officers over.

"What are you doing here? You're ruining everything!" a woman's voice hissed.

"Me? What about you, where's Joseph?" the second voice sounded like Amanda's.

"We need to try again later."

"No, Sonja, I paid good money to have him now!" Amanda shrieked, her voice rising a full octave.

Mark nodded. So, it was the American assassin whose name Liam had gotten who was behind all this. With the appearance of the snake he'd begun to wonder if it was one of the others on the list.

He lifted his hand and let it fall and the officers flowed into the room. "Freeze, police!" the lead one yelled as he flipped on the light switch.

Mark entered the room just as Sonja spun Amanda around to use as a human shield.

"I told you that you were crazy to want to take him here," Sonja hissed.

"And you promised me he would be mine before he married that tramp," Amanda wailed.

Sonja was backing up, her left arm wrapped around Amanda's chest with a knife held against her. In her right hand she held a gun aimed at Mark. She was heading for the door behind her that led out toward the parking lot. If she got through it, they might lose her.

"What do you want me to do?" Liam asked softly.

"Do you have a clean shot?"

"Murky."

The two women were co-conspirators, even though one had now turned on the other.

"Take it."

Liam fired and a moment later Sonja dropped like a stone, a bullet hole in the middle of her forehead. Amanda fell with her and Mark rushed forward, kicking both the gun and the knife away from her.

"He's mine!" Amanda shrieked even as another officer rushed forward and handcuffed her. He pulled her to her feet and Amanda stared at Mark in rage. "How dare you come between us?"

"You hired her to kidnap him for you," he said, pointing to Sonja.

"Yes, I had to sell my house to afford it, but I'd do it all again in a heartbeat," Amanda raved.

"And you paid her to kill Geanie so she'd be out of the way permanently."

"Oh no, I couldn't afford to have Geanie killed. Sonja said it would be another five hundred thousand for that, and I just didn't have that kind of money. Besides, I knew that if I could just get him alone, away from her, I could make him see reason," Amanda said, her eyes shining with madness.

"Right, so you both just wanted us to think it was about Geanie," Mark said.

Her face twisted in fury. "That witch kept me from getting my invitation. He wanted me here. Joseph invited me. *Me*."

"No, *we* invited you," Mark said. "Joseph didn't want anything to do with you."

"It's not true," she said, her lips trembling.

"Take her away," Mark said to the officer.

"He loves me, me! You'll see! One of these days he'll come to his senses," Amanda shrieked all the way out of the building.

"Great shot," he complimented Liam as the other officer stepped forward.

"Thank you," Liam said, looking like he was going to be ill.

Mark clapped him on the shoulder. "It's okay," he said.

Liam just nodded mutely.

~

Jeremiah set Cindy down and then struggled to his feet. Mark had chased the assassin, but something didn't seem right to him.

"Where's the main power shut off for the building?" he asked Cindy.

"Um, It's on the outside wall, far left side, by the library."

"And the circuit breakers?"

"Back wall, far corner."

Whoever had cut the power wouldn't have had time to get into position to hit him in the back of the head just now. So, either the assassin had Amanda or another person helping them or they had a whole different problem.

He had a moment of indecision as he tried to decide whether Cindy would be safer with him or away from him. He finally pulled her back inside and thrust her into Dave and Joseph's arms. The rest of the wedding party was hunkered down at the front of the sanctuary. They grabbed her and pulled her into their midst.

"No one gets near her until this is done. Understand?" Jeremiah hissed.

"No one," Dave reiterated.

Jeremiah took off back through the side door and made it outside, then started running around the building. He could see the main power shut off and had nearly reached it when the hair on the back of his neck stood up.

He spun in midstride and grabbed the man who was charging him, slamming him to the ground and pinning him there with an arm across his throat as he knelt on his chest.

Instinctually he knew this was the man who had bombed the bridal shop and left the black rose and the message for Mark. He was middle eastern, well-dressed, and even though he was in the weaker position he was smiling.

"Why try to kill Cindy?" he demanded, grateful that no one was around to hear.

"She is your woman. That is reason enough."

Jeremiah didn't bother arguing with him, telling him that she wasn't his. Instead he asked, "You know who I am?"

"Yes. So did the man whose dog you now have."

"Did you kill him?" Jeremiah asked.

The man's grin widened. "One of my brothers was responsible for that. The important thing is we know where you are now, we know who you love. And no matter what happens here, you will die."

Jeremiah heard a gunshot. One way or another everything was ending now. "How many of you are there?"

"Enough."

"Who are you?"

"You do not recognize me?" the man asked.

Jeremiah didn't, but he didn't say anything.

"Of course, how could you?" the man said. "You never look to the left or the right."

"I will hunt down all your brothers," Jeremiah promised.

The man just kept grinning. "No need. They will be coming for you. Not today. Not tomorrow. But soon."

Jeremiah heard the sound of approaching footsteps.

The man on the ground kept talking. "And I promise you that when they find you-"

Jeremiah snapped his neck and stood up. A moment later Mark and Liam came into view.

"What happened here?" Mark asked.

"I think he must have surprised whoever shut off the electricity," Jeremiah said. "I checked him for a pulse and everything. He seems to be dead."

"Looking like that? I'd be shocked if he wasn't." Mark sighed. "I hope Joseph or Geanie weren't good friends of his."

"I don't recognize him, so I'm guessing not," Jeremiah said.

"Good. Now, let's get the lights on and then you come with me."

Mark led Jeremiah back into the sanctuary a minute later where people were happy to have the lights restored. Mark and Jeremiah walked up to the front and at their approach the rest of the bridal party stood.

"It's over," Mark said softly.

And then they were all hugging and crying together. It lasted for several seconds before Mark finally broke free and borrowed the microphone from the bewildered minister. He looked out over the assembled wedding guests, most of whom seemed to be finding their way back to their seats if they had gotten up.

"Everyone okay? Yes? Great. Then, everyone take your seats and let's get ready to do this all again."

~

Geanie and Cindy headed for the room they had changed in earlier. It was a miracle, but in less than five minutes they'd managed to trade dresses. As everyone huddled up at the back door of the sanctuary Geanie told everyone to ditch their masks for the ceremony, but to make sure to keep them for the reception.

As Geanie and Joseph exchanged their vows Cindy felt a tear roll down her cheek. All the fear and the death and the chaos was over and the wedding was happening and it was beautiful.

She noticed the other bridesmaids dabbing at their eyes, too. Tears were streaming openly down Dave's cheeks and he didn't seem to care who saw them. As for Geanie and Joseph, they were both smiling like they'd never stop. Cindy said a prayer for them and their marriage that it might be true.

When the ceremony was over the guests started heading to the reception location while the wedding party stayed behind to pose for photos for the photographer. The man was still rattled from everything that had happened and distraught over having not been allowed to be present earlier for photos.

When it was finally time to take a group shot with the whole wedding party together Cindy held up her hand over the couple's heads and Jeremiah high-fived her. That, at least, got a smile out of the photographer.

The limo ride to the reception was filled with excited laughter that was completely different in feel and nature to the nervous laughter that had filled the limo on the way to the church.

When they entered the banquet hall Cindy was thrilled to see that all of the guests had already gotten into the spirit of the evening and were wearing their masks.

The reception line was interminable, but at least people were respectful and kept moving through quickly. Cindy's feet were hurting by the time they finally were able to sit down and start eating. All around her was color and pageantry but she took a few moments to just breathe and focus on her food. It was all a bit overwhelming but once she had cleaned half her plate she was starting to feel much better.

~

Joseph and Geanie had their first dance. The dance following everyone was encouraged to join in and Jeremiah took Cindy's hand and led her to the dance floor. The music playing was "Point of No Return" from Phantom of the Opera. Jeremiah held Cindy in his arms and together they moved across the dance floor. He couldn't help but listen to the lyrics to the song even as his own emotions collided within him. A week ago he had still been planning to leave before things got more complicated between him and Cindy.

Now that was impossible. He couldn't leave, because his past had finally caught up with him and he wouldn't abandon her to it. The time had come to tell her the truth, no matter what it cost him. Not the whole truth, but what she needed to know. She deserved to know at least part of it. But not now, not during Geanie and Joseph's much deserved celebration and not during this dance which he wished would never end.

Cindy leaned her head against his chest and it made him ache deep inside. He loved her. There was no denying it. When they had been standing in front of the minister and she had been reciting vows to him part of him had wished that it was all real.

He wasn't sure how or when it had all happened, but it had. Two years ago she was the pretty stranger whom he'd see in the neighboring parking lot when he got into work sometimes, nothing more. Now she was everything, and he had thoughts about her that he couldn't control, feelings that were getting harder and harder to just ignore. He cursed his past which kept them apart.

"Is everything alright?" she whispered against his shoulder, as though sensing the struggle he was going through.

He tightened his arms around her. He could have this moment, he would give it to himself. "At this moment, everything is perfect," he said.

20

Mark was sitting next to Traci. The reception was still in full swing and everyone seemed to be having a magnificent time. He had to admit that seeing all the dancers in their masks whirling by was a sight to behold.

"If you don't finish your cake, I'm stealing it," Traci warned.

"It is really good," Mark said with a grin, "but I'd sacrifice my dessert to you any day."

Joseph walked over to them, a grin on his face. He sat down in one of the empty chairs. "Thank you both for everything," he said.

"Just doing my job," Mark said, his reflex response.

"No, you went far above and beyond your job. And, it certainly isn't Traci's job."

"That's true," Traci said with a laugh.

"Here, this is for you," Joseph said, handing Mark and Traci an envelope.

"What is it?" Mark asked.

"Two weeks, all expense paid trip to Tahiti. Your plane leaves tomorrow. I've made all the arrangements."

"What?" Traci gasped.

"Liam helped me clear it with your captain. He said as long as the case was solved, you were free to take some of your vacation time. I wanted to surprise Geanie with our honeymoon destination, but I wasn't one-hundred percent sure what her surprises were for me and so I kept my options open. I booked one trip to Paris and the other to Tahiti, making the arrangements in such a way that I could easily switch the names on one vacation. I figured we'd give the other one away, and the two of you certainly deserve it. Now, I have to get back to my bride."

When Joseph had walked away Traci punched Mark lightly in the arm. "Bet you're glad I volunteered to be a bridesmaid now," she said.

"I am, I really am," he said, still feeling slightly dazed.

"You promised me a vacation after this," she said with a happy smile.

"I did. I just didn't think it would all work out quite so well," he said, tucking the envelope into his jacket. "You know the thing about Joseph?"

"What?"

"He's really down-to-earth and easy going, but when he decides to make a big gesture, he makes a really big gesture." He turned and smiled at Traci. "Well, we have some packing to do, but right now would you care to dance?"

"I'd love to," she said with a smile.

He took her hand and led her onto the dance floor.

~

Cindy felt a surge of relief as they saw Joseph and Geanie off. Once they were gone she and the others went back inside. It looked like the party was going to continue well into the night.

She danced several more times with Jeremiah until her feet were so sore she could barely stand. When the party finally broke up just after midnight she helped with the clean-up efforts along with everyone else.

The wedding party made it back to Joseph's, but instead of heading straight for bed, exhausted as they all were, they congregated in the living room to relive everything that happened.

Cindy had to retell the events at the church since most of the group hadn't seen what had actually happened. It was nearly four a.m. by the time she was in her room. The second her head hit the pillow she was asleep.

The next morning was more bittersweet than she would have thought as everyone started packing up to go home. She realized with a start that she was going to miss the camaraderie of the past week.

Jeremiah dropped her at her house, but they made plans to have a late lunch together and decompress some more.

After dumping everything in her room Cindy looked around the house and it suddenly hit her that she no longer had a roommate. She felt tears sting her eyes. She had enjoyed having Geanie as a roommate and she was going to miss her.

She wandered into her office and sat down at her computer. She pulled up her email and gasped. There was a message from Gerald that looked to have been sent the morning he was attacked. It had three attachments. With a shaking hand she clicked on the first one.

~

Mark was sitting at his desk feeling like he was drowning in paperwork. He rubbed his eyes, wishing he could just slough all of it off onto Liam. Liam had his own stack of paperwork, though.

He saw someone walking toward him and he turned and was surprised to see that it was Cindy. Without preamble she sat down in the chair next to his desk.

"Can I do something for you?" he asked.

"Actually, I can do something for you," she said, handing him three sheets of paper.

"What are these?"

"When I checked my computer this morning I found that Gerald had emailed these to me the morning he was attacked."

The top one was a birth certificate for a boy, Andrew John Matthews. His parents were listed as Tobi A. Matthews and Sarah Matthews.

He glanced up. "Andrew John Matthews. Do you think...is this Paul?" he asked, finding it suddenly hard to speak.

"Look at the other two pages," she said.

He turned to the next one. It was an elementary school record for Andrew John Matthews, age 7. In the field reserved for parent or legal guardian it listed Simon A. Matthews and a notation next to it read 'Grandfather'. With a shaking hand he turned to the third picture which looked like it was from a school yearbook. The seven year old boy who was staring back at him was Paul. He'd bet his life on it.

The papers slipped from his fingers and fell onto the desk.

"The school is in New Orleans. I looked it up, along with Simon A. Matthews. Apparently he was a pastor, very famous at the time. He was murdered the same year as that school record."

"And the boy?" Mark whispered.

"I couldn't find a reference to him in any of the articles I read. The killer was never caught, although there was strong speculation that Simon knew his attacker because there was no sign of forced entry. He was killed just a couple of weeks before Matthew Tobias showed up in Righteousness. Also, Matthew Tobias is an anagram of Tobi A. Matthews. Not even an overly clever one at that."

"But just enough to never raise any red flags," Mark said.

"Exactly."

He felt like he couldn't think straight, like every time he tried to latch on to a thought it slipped away from him. "I don't think there's any doubt that Paul was this boy Andrew John."

"Neither do I. And I'm positive Gerald wouldn't have sent me these documents if he wasn't also sure."

"Okay, so, walk me through what you think happened," he said.

Cindy took a deep breath and leaned forward. "I think Tobi had a son named Andrew. He wasn't a good father, a criminal. Tobi's father Simon is a pastor, an upstanding pillar of the community. He takes the boy to raise. Tobi eventually gets his revenge, killing his father and taking back his son who doesn't want to go with him. Tobi moves the two of them cross country to Righteousness where he changes his name and keeps the boy hidden from the townsfolk, probably a prisoner since Andrew is upset that his father killed his grandfather. When he's exposed as a criminal there, he moves again, this time to California where he just goes by the name Matthew. He and his followers move on to crimes such as kidnapping. His son, Andrew, befriends one of the young victims. When Andrew is finally able to escape, he takes the other boy's identity, ensuring that he can never be sent back to his father, a man he knows to be a monster."

"And people believe because they want to, because the boys look similar enough and because Andrew knows so much about Paul's life. Only, the new Paul has grown to hate religion because of what happened to him and his grandfather and how his father has twisted it. He also is afraid of the word 'Righteousness' because it was the town he was taken to as a captive immediately after seeing his father murder his grandfather," Mark said.

"Exactly." Cindy took a deep breath and then continued. "The cult is massacred and Andrew thinks he is safe until years later when someone comes looking for the truth."

"What made him think Gerald would find out anything about him, though?"

"I don't think he was worried about Gerald finding out the truth about him. I think he was worried about Gerald writing too much about the cult in the same book that he was talking about the Passion Week Killer and the police involved in that investigation."

"Because the name Paul Dryer might be noticed by someone with more than a passing interest in that cult."

"Someone murdered those cult members and buried their bodies. That someone would have also known that the real Paul Dryer was dead."

"And so Andrew becomes afraid that someone will put two and two together, and come back, looking for him," Mark said.

"Exactly. And I have a pretty good idea who killed the cultists and who our friend was afraid would return to the area."

"His father."

Cindy nodded. "When Gerald called he had already sent these documents to me. He said he had shocking news. He didn't say anything about Paul, what his real name was, anything. No, he said, 'Matthew is'. I think he was about to say that Matthew is alive."

"And if so, maybe, just maybe he's been hiding out back in good old New Orleans where this all started."

"Which is why Gerald is still in danger," Cindy said. She took a deep breath. "What do you think of my theory?"

"I like it enough to almost call it fact without any other investigating at all," Mark admitted.

"So, there's a mass murderer in New Orleans. What do we do about it?" she asked.

He looked sharply at her. "We? We don't do anything. I'll hand over what I have to the New Orleans police and let them take it from there. I just got word from them about an hour ago that it looks like Gerald is going to pull through, so hopefully he can help them as well."

"But-"

"No buts," he said holding up his hand. "This is out of our hands now. We found out what we set out to. Thank you for that. In exactly six hours, though, Traci and I are on our way to Tahiti. I suggest you take some time off, too. We all need it. Now I've got to get this finished so I can get home and help Traci with the packing," he said.

Cindy stood up. "Okay, I've got to meet Jeremiah for a late lunch, but I thought you'd like to see all this," Cindy said.

"Yes, thank you. I really do appreciate it."

She gave him a small smile before leaving.

Mark picked up the picture of Andrew, aged seven, and leaned back in his chair. He felt like he was staring into his old partner's eyes all over again. "I'm sorry about everything that happened to you," he whispered. "At least, now, I know your name."

~

Cindy met Jeremiah at his house. When he opened the door he smiled at her faintly, but it never reached his eyes and she felt a chill touch her.

"Come in," he said.

She followed him inside and he closed the door. "So, where are we going?" she asked.

"I decided to cook. I thought we could talk...privately," he said.

Again, something in his demeanor chilled her. He was making her nervous and she wished she knew why.

"Sounds good," she said, cheerily, following him into the kitchen. "You'll never guess what I found when I checked my email."

"What?"

"A message from Gerald. By the way Mark said he got a call and it looks like Gerald is going to pull through."

"That's great news. So, what did the message say?"

Cindy spent the next several minutes filling him in while he finished up making lunch which was salmon with an amazing smelling sauce and Caesar salads. By the time they were sitting down to eat she had brought him up to speed.

"So, one mystery solved," he said.

"And another one revealed."

He gave her a fleeting smile.

They began to eat and as the meal progressed Cindy became more and more uncomfortable. She made small talk, chatted about the crazy things at the reception, but it was hard to get more than one word answers out of Jeremiah.

Finally she pushed her plate back and turned to him. "Okay, what's wrong? You're starting to scare me."

He turned his chair to face her. "I need to tell you something," he said.

"Okay."

"We know that Amanda hired Sonja to kidnap Joseph."

"Yes."

"But that doesn't explain the attacks on Geanie, the car, the bridal shop, etc."

"I figure Sonja just saw it as a bonus."

"That man you saw at the bridal shop and then again at Rue de Main, you remember him?"

"Of course. I figure he was one of the people that Sonja hired, just like those tailors."

He shook his head. "No, he had nothing to do with Sonja or Amanda."

Cindy blinked in surprise. "Then who was he?"

Jeremiah took a ragged breath. "That's not important. What's important is what he was doing. He was the one responsible for the bridal shop, the car, the snake, and the black rose."

"Why?" Cindy asked bewildered. She couldn't figure out who would want to harm Geanie and why Jeremiah hadn't told Mark any of this.

"He was never after Geanie," Jeremiah said, his face contorting slightly.

"What are you talking about? Of course he was."

Jeremiah shook his head. "No, he was after you."

Cindy stared at him as his words sunk in. The first time she'd seen him she had been the one wearing the wedding dress, not Geanie. Was it possible he had thought she was getting married? But that still made no sense. "Why?" she finally asked. "I've never seen him before. I don't even know who he is. Why would he possibly want to hurt me?"

Jeremiah dropped his eyes to the ground and it was as though she could literally see him struggling to answer her. Finally he looked back up and there was an intensity in his eyes she'd only glimpsed a couple of times before. "He thought that hurting you would hurt me and he was right."

"I don't understand."

"He believed that you and I were...together. He planned to kill you because of me."

"Why?"

"Because I'm not the man you think I am," he said, standing abruptly and pacing across the room.

Cindy felt like she couldn't catch her breath. "This has something to do with your past, doesn't it?"

"It has everything to do with it," he said, and she noticed with a start that his voice was suddenly heavily accented. She knew he'd grown up in Israel, but he'd never really spoken with much of an accent. It often made it easy to forget that he was from a different country, a different culture. Hearing the accent now just brought it back home that she knew almost nothing about his past, nothing from before that day they'd met over a dead body in the sanctuary.

She stood even though waves of fear were rolling through her and she walked over to him. She grabbed his hands and forced him to face her. "You need to tell me the truth," she said. "I've known for a long time you were hiding something from me, and I was okay with that. I figured you'd tell me whatever it was when you were ready. Clearly, though, in light of what you've just said you need to tell me now. You must think so, too, otherwise we wouldn't be here."

"You have to understand, I never expected any of this. I never expected...you."

"I know, but I'm here, and clearly there's something we need to deal with."

"It could get you killed," he said, his voice dropping to a whisper which was hard to understand with the thickness of the accent.

"And apparently, not knowing can get me killed as well. Jeremiah, you have to trust me."

He laughed, a hard, bitter sound.

"What's so funny?" she asked.

He looked her in the eyes for the first time since she had gotten to his house. "That's not even my name."

She felt the world coming apart around her, but she forced herself to stand there, holding his hands, looking into his eyes.

"What is your name?" she asked, her voice trembling so hard she could barely get the words out.

"I can't tell you that," he said, shaking his head.

"Why did you choose that name?" she asked.

"I didn't. It was chosen for me."

"By who?" she asked, her heart pounding in her chest. Somehow she knew that what he was going to say next was going to change everything.

He took a deep breath and she could see the conflict, the struggle in his eyes. Finally, he said, in a clear, strong voice, "HaMossad leModi'in uleTafkidim Meyuḥadim. Or, as you would know it, the Mossad."

Debbie Viguié is the New York Times Bestselling author of more than three dozen novels including the *Wicked* series, the *Crusade* series and the *Wolf Springs Chronicles* series co-authored with Nancy Holder. Debbie also writes thrillers including *The Psalm 23 Mysteries,* the *Kiss* trilogy, and the *Witch Hunt* trilogy. When Debbie isn't busy writing she enjoys spending time with her husband, Scott, visiting theme parks. They live in Florida with their cat, Schrödinger.

CPSIA information can be obtained
at www.ICGtesting.com
Printed in the USA
LVHW010006071222
734695LV00004B/333